www.AshleyEmmaAuthor.com

Check out my author Facebook page to see rare photos from when I lived with the Amish in Unity, Maine. Just Search for 'Ashley Emma, author and publisher' on Facebook.

Join my free Facebook group 'The Amish Book Club' where I share free Amish books weekly!

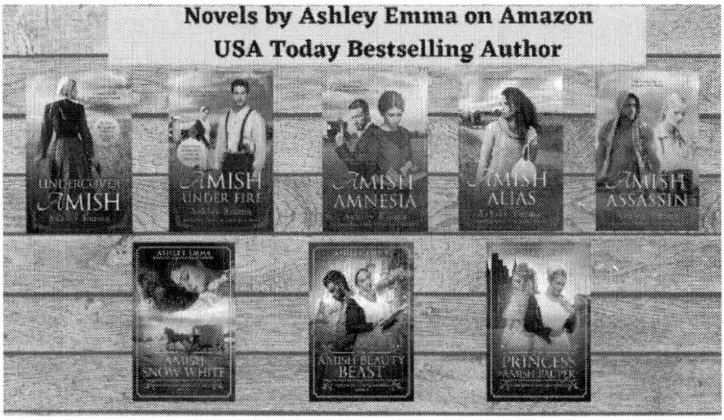
Novels by Ashley Emma on Amazon
USA Today Bestselling Author
UNDERCOVER AMISH
AMISH UNDER FIRE
AMISH AMNESIA
AMISH ALIAS
AMISH ASSASSIN
AMISH SNOW WHITE
AMISH BEAUTY BEAST
PRINCESS AMISH PAUPER

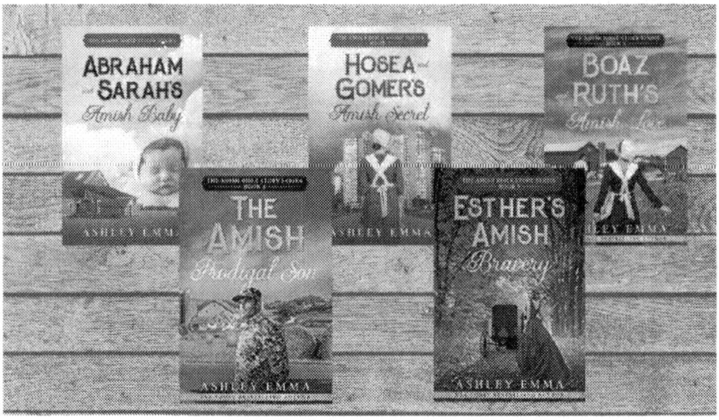
ABRAHAM SARAH'S Amish Baby
HOSEA GOMER'S Amish Secret
BOAZ RUTH'S
THE AMISH Prodigal Son
ESTHER'S AMISH Bravery
ASHLEY EMMA

THE AMISH SCHOOLTEACHER'S ESCAPE

THE AMISH SCHOOLTEACHER'S ESCAPE

Prequel to The Covert Police Detectives Unit Series

Ashley Emma

CONTENTS

CHAPTER ONE

Martha's eyes slowly opened, but it was so early that the room was still dark. She stayed in bed for a moment, wishing she could spend more time there. But as she heard the movements in the next room, she knew her day had begun.

She dressed for the day in a blue dress and black apron. She packed her long dark hair in a bun, as always, then covered it with her white prayer *kapp* and grabbed her brown bag, which contained all she needed for the day.

"Good morning, *Maam*," Martha murmured as she stepped into the kitchen.

Her stepmother, Barbara, only glared at her, then turned her attention back to the bowl of vegetables she was chopping.

"Want me to help you with that?" Martha asked.

"No. I don't need your help. Go find something else to do," Barbara snapped. She turned her head away from Martha, her graying brown hair mostly hidden by her prayer *kapp.*

Martha's stepmother, Barbara, a widow and mother of two sons, married Martha's father after he became a widower. Martha was his only child. Martha's father had told Barbara's sons that they could call him *Daed,* and he soon took on the role of their new loving stepfather. However, Barbara had not extended a similar invitation or motherly love to Martha.

Martha shrugged off her stepmother's cold behavior and went about her morning duties.

"Good morning, *Daed,*" Martha greeted her father.

"Good morning, my dear." He kissed her on the forehead, his long white beard tickling her cheek. His kind gray eyes lit up when he smiled.

Martha's two teenage stepbrothers, Neil and Richard, stomped downstairs and came bounding into the kitchen.

"Good morning, darlings," Barbara cooed, giving them each a kiss on the cheek. "Did you sleep well?"

"Yes, *Maam*," they both replied. Barbara adored her sons, but Martha had no idea why Barbara disliked her so much.

"Neil, Richard, Martha, I need your help moving those boxes of supplies from my buggy that I picked up early this morning. Let's go do it now before breakfast," *Daed* said.

Martha and her stepbrothers followed *Daed* outside. It was still quite early in the morning, but the community had awoken. The rays of the morning sun crept over the hills, showering its blessings on the town.

She waved to her neighbors as they stepped out of their houses to do their chores. The chickens also called out their greetings as they pecked on grains of corn.

Martha turned and let out a long breath of frustration when she saw Jake Sullivan walking by their house.

Jake Sullivan was a tall, well-built man in his late twenties who lived down the lane. He was handsome and a good worker, admired by almost everyone, especially the young women in the community. Ever since Martha was a teenager, his eyes had been set on her, and it was only a matter of time before he asked to court her—something which she awaited so she could turn him down and deflate his ego. She certainly had, and he had never let it go.

"Hello, there!" Jake called. "Need some help with those boxes?"

"That would be great, if you have a moment, Jake," *Daed* replied.

"Of course. Happy to help," Jake said politely and sauntered over to them, flashing Martha a dashing grin as he passed her. "How are you on this fine day, Martha?" His eyes looked her up and down hungrily, and she glared at him for being so crude.

"Well enough, thank you." She tried not to cringe.

"Guess I walked by at just the right time. I'm always happy to help someone in need," he said smugly.

She willed herself to not roll her eyes as he walked over to her father and picked up a box.

The men made small talk as they moved the boxes into the barn, and as Martha turned, she looked up at the house. Barbara was standing in the kitchen window, watching the men—especially Jake—and smiling. Barbara caught Martha's eye and glared at her before pivoting away and drawing the curtains.

Martha frowned. How could her family not see right through him? Jake was always quick to help others, that was for sure, but to Martha, it was obvious that he was arrogant. Every time she was around Jake, he made her feel completely uncomfortable. And right now, all she wanted to do was get away from him.

As the last box was unloaded, she hurried back into the house to help her stepmother finish making breakfast. Right now, she'd rather be alone with her stepmother than be around Jake, and that was saying something.

She had no idea what she had done to upset her stepmother, but Barbara had only tolerated Martha from the moment she had married her father. Martha had tried all she could to make her stepmother like her, but all her attempts had failed; nothing she did would ever make her stepmother love her.

Her father and stepbrothers came back inside and they all sat at the breakfast table.

Daed proclaimed, "What a beautiful day the Lord has made. We are so blessed to live in such a wonderful place. We should make the most of today, as always."

They bowed their heads for a silent prayer, then devoured the eggs, biscuits, gravy, and fruit that Martha and Barbara had prepared.

"*Daed,* may I leave work early today?" Neil, Martha's younger stepbrother, asked. They both worked with their father on the family farm that sold produce to local supermarkets.

"Why, so you can go see Betty Graber again? Neil has a *girlfriend.*" Richard, Martha's youngest stepbrother, laughed.

Neil elbowed him and mumbled, "I do not. Not yet. I haven't officially asked her yet." He blushed and added, "Anyway, her parents invited me over for dinner this evening and asked me to help with some things before we eat."

"I suppose that would be all right. If you get all your work done for the day before leaving."

"Thank you," Neil said.

"And what about you, Martha? How are things going with you and Jake?" Barbara asked.

"Nothing is going on with Jake and me. I really don't have an interest in him, not romantically. Not at all. He's only a friend, if that." Martha hated to even use that word in association with him.

Barbara shook her head, her blue eyes flashing. "Well, he's a fine man, and you're not getting any younger."

Martha looked down at her plate, biting back a retort. "He's not the right man for me. I don't have any feelings for him. Also, there's something about him that makes me uneasy."

"Oh, please." Barbara waved a hand dismissively. "Many girls in the community would be happy to have him interested in them. Everyone here knows he's a kind young man."

Kind was definitely not the word Martha would use to describe him. She tried as much as possible to not be around him, but of late, he was always popping up unexpectedly.

"Martha will fall in love when she's ready and when God brings the right man into her life, Barbara," *Daed* said gently, glancing at Martha and giving her a small smile. Martha smiled back, grateful for his words.

After breakfast, *Daed* and the boys headed outside the same time as Martha was also leaving the house to go to school. She hurried down the lane to the schoolhouse where she taught the children of the community. It was a job she thoroughly loved, and it was also a way for her to get out of the house.

Unity, Maine, was a relatively small Amish community. However, like all Amish communities, they were one big family who worked together for their common good.

Martha had lived in the community all her life. She loved the people who she had grown up with; they were a larger part of her family even if they were not related by blood. She had heard of people leaving the community, and she could not help but wonder why. She read books about the outside world, and although she was intrigued by it, she was content to stay here.

However, she was beginning to feel a sense of lack in her life.

She loved the Amish way of life, and she loved her community. She wanted to live here forever. But there was something missing in her life.

As she continued walking, she approached the school. The schoolhouse was also the church building—a simple, two-story wooden structure.

Unlike many Amish communities that hosted church in people's homes, they had built their own church building instead.

One half of the second floor was the school room, and the other half was the church sanctuary. It was divided by a collapsible room divider to make more room when needed, such as for a wedding. They set out tables on the first floor for potluck lunches after church on Sundays.

She knew each of her students by name, and she loved all of them. They were so kind and innocent; they were happy children who she was going to miss when their school education ended at eighth grade. She taught them all together in the same classroom, which was decorated with alphabet letters, charts, and the students' artwork. There were also large shelves with books and supplies.

The classroom was empty when she walked in, just as she expected, since she was early as usual. She opened the windows, ushering the morning light in. In a few minutes, the chatters of the children filled the room.

"Good morning, children," Martha called.

"Good morning, Miss Martha," they chorused back at her.

The morning passed as she concentrated on the children, taking them through the subjects for the day. After lunch, the children went out to play. Martha sat at her desk, eating fruits and vegetables from local farms and her homemade bread.

"Hi, Miss Martha. How are you doing today?"

Martha looked up to see one of her students, Timothy, smiling at her.

"I'm well, Timothy. Thank you."

"You look a little sad. Are you sure?" He cocked his head to the side.

"Oh, yes. I am just deep in thought. I have a lot on my mind."

"If you pray and ask God, he will show you what to do."

Martha grinned. "You're right, Timothy. Thank you for reminding me."

"Well, I have some good news. I have a new older brother. He just moved here, and he's the best. He plays catch and board games with me, and he's really nice and funny. His name is Isaiah. I bet you'd like him."

"He sounds like a wonderful person. I'd be happy to meet him. Maybe we will see him at church on Sunday."

"Come on, Timothy!" the other boys called, and he scampered outside to join them.

The sounds of the children's feet coming back in drew her from the conflicts running through her mind. It was later in the afternoon when she waved goodbye to the children as they ran home. She returned to the classroom to prepare for her class the following day.

"Martha."

Martha froze, then whirled around and looked to the doorway of the classroom. Jake stood there, staring at her.

"Jake, what are you doing here?" Martha asked, pretending not to be flustered.

Jake smiled, causing Martha to cringe and look away. "Are you done for the day?" he asked.

She put her hands on her hips, anger flaring within her. Who did he think he was, showing up here like this? "You should go. It's not appropriate for you to be here with no one else around."

"I just want to walk you home. What's the harm in that?"

She rolled her eyes. "I'll walk home alone, thank you."

"I'm not taking no for an answer."

The anger returning, she pursed her lips and let out a short breath. This man was insufferable.

She didn't want to walk home with Jake, but she knew he wouldn't leave. "Fine."

She filled her arms with her bag and books. Just as she expected, he didn't even bother to help her with her things. And this was the man whose praises her stepmother sang? A man who wouldn't even help her carry her books?

"What are your plans for the evening?" Jake asked as they stepped outside into the yard.

"Umm... I have some chores to do for my stepmother," Martha said. She knew lying was a sin, but there was no other excuse she could think of. Besides, she was sure she could find some chores to do, which she would much rather do than see him.

Jake laughed as they began to walk to her house. "I'm sure your stepmother would not mind me taking you out. She is rather fond of me."

Too fond of him, in her opinion. Her stepmother never failed to speak highly of him and tell her how blessed she was to have a man like Jake shower his attention on her.

"No thanks," Martha said. "Sorry, but I have no interest in going out with you."

Jake frowned in displeasure, obviously not used to being turned down. "You know, when we get married, you will have to stop teaching at the school because you'll be spending your time taking care of me, our children, and our house."

Her mouth fell open in surprise. His words sent a dreaded chill through her spine, quickly followed by a blast of more anger. The last thing she wanted was Jake as a husband. If she married him, Martha suspected he would make sure she obeyed his every wish; she would have no sense of freedom.

"*When* we get married?" She let out a humorless laugh. "You think you can win me over just like that? You're not as charming as you think. I am not going to marry you."

"Excuse me?" Jake retorted.

A young man came around the side of the schoolhouse, someone she'd never seen before. He was walking with Joseph Gray, a local carpenter and one of the church ministers.

Anger suddenly washed over Jake's face, and his fingers clenched as he followed her gaze. Her heart began to race as she stared at the mysterious man who stood outside the schoolhouse.

Who was he?

He was tall. His eyes were blue, and he had dark brown, wavy hair. There was something calm about him, which made her feel safe and peaceful, even at a distance.

"Who's that?" she whispered, gesturing to the young man.

"Nobody you should know," Jake snapped, his hand encircling her wrist as he dragged her towards her home. She jerked free, swatting his hands away.

"Let go of me!" she shouted.

"Martha, what's wrong with you?" he demanded.

"Is there a problem?" Joseph Gray asked, quickly striding over to them, followed by the new young man. Jake let go of her.

"No," Jake retorted, still looking at Martha.

"It seems like there's a problem," the young man insisted. Martha's eyes darted to the stranger, and his gaze locked with hers.

"Do not touch her," the minister commanded. "She clearly doesn't want you to, and touching a woman against her will is not tolerated here."

The young man narrowed his eyes at Jake, stepping closer to him. "You should learn some respect for women."

Jake glowered at him. "Leave us alone. This is none of your business."

"It's my business when I see a man mistreating a woman, and you were being rough with her," the young man retorted. "She asked you to let go."

"Gentleman, please." Joseph Gray raised his hands. "There is no need to argue. Jake, what you did was wrong. Step away from Martha." When Jake hesitated, the minister added, "Now, Jake."

Jake turned to Martha. "This is not over," he spat out, then stomped away like an angry toddler throwing a tantrum. She half-expected him to throw himself on the ground and pound his fists on the grass, screaming, and she almost laughed at the image.

"Thank you," Martha said to the stranger and the minister.

"No need to thank us," the minister said. "He shouldn't have done that. I hope he doesn't bother you again. If he does, the elders will deal with him."

"Thank you again." Martha's eyes settled on the young man once again.

"This is Isaiah," Joseph said. "Isaiah, this is Martha, the schoolteacher."

"Nice to meet you, Martha." Isaiah tipped his head toward her, and she detected a hint of an accent, but she couldn't tell where he was from.

"You as well." She smiled.

"We have to get going. Have a nice day, Martha," the minister said, and the two men walked toward the church.

Martha watched them, puzzled. Who was this Isaiah, and why had Jake been so upset with him?

CHAPTER TWO

"Have you heard about that new young man who has moved here? His name is Isaiah," Martha said to the family at dinner two nights later.

News traveled fast in the community. It was no surprise.

"Actually, yes. I was visiting Mrs. Johnson today, and she told me that once, in his youthful age, Joseph Gray strayed from the Lord. During his *rumspringa*, he was with a woman. He finally realized he was on the wrong path and returned," Barbara told her.

Richard added, "I heard it was only recently that one of the church elders, Joseph Gray, found out he had a grown-up son who came here looking for him."

"Why is he here?" Neil asked.

"Isaiah is here to be with his father," *Daed* explained. "That is all."

Barbara's eyes narrowed in suspicion. "Really? That sounds strange. An outsider coming to join us is not something that happens every day. I am sure he will be out of here in no time. This must be an experimental phase for him."

"I don't think so. I spoke with Joseph, and he told me the boy has grown up Amish in another community in Wisconsin," Martha's father explained.

"I still do not like him." Barbara folded her arms across her chest. "Boys, I don't want you spending time with him. You are both such fine, godly young men, and I don't want that to change. Martha, you should avoid him too."

"I disagree," *Daed* countered. "We should welcome him. The Lord brought Isaiah here to us. This is the first time in a long while that I've seen Joseph really happy. All these years, now he seems complete. I even heard him whistling a tune. The son he never knew he had is here. What father wouldn't be happy? And he's an intelligent boy. We have heard good news about him even before we knew he was Joseph's son."

"I still do not like him," Barbara insisted.

"The Lord tells us to love everyone, and that includes him. What's more, Isaiah's a part of our church family," *Daed* said.

Martha had barely spoken two words to Isaiah, but she could tell that he was kind. She was happy for Joseph; he was a good man who always had a smile for her.

Timothy was one of her favorite children in school, and he showed good behavior, reflecting his upright upbringing by his parents.

The following Saturday, after the morning chores were done and breakfast had been cleaned up, Barbara called out to Martha, "Get ready. We're going to the farmer's market."

The buggy ride to the market was quiet. She had learned a long time ago that Barbara was interested in no chitchat with her. Barbara preferred Martha to always be quiet, saying it was a sign of good upbringing which her mother had never instilled in her. Instead, her mother had showed her that Martha could speak with her about anything and that she should speak up for herself.

The sight of the farmer's market made Martha light up. She was going to see her Amish friends, Catherine and Antonia, who helped their parents sell their produce from their farm. She rarely got to see them because of their busy lives. The buggy halted, and Martha got out and ruffled the mane of the chestnut horse, which pulled the buggy.

"Stick close to me," Barbara warned, climbing out of the buggy. "If you stray, I won't wait for you. I'll go home without you."

Martha gulped, her plans of meeting up with her friends ruined. She knew Barbara would leave her behind; she had done so before, leaving Martha to walk all the way home.

The women went from stall to stall, shopping. Martha carried the basket, and soon it was full, its weight bearing on her.

"Martha!" Catherine stood a few stalls away, waving to Martha.

Martha smiled at her friend Catherine. "Can I go say hi to her?" she asked Barbara expectantly.

Barbara paused in contemplation. "Five minutes."

Martha ran to Catherine and hugged her. "How have you been?"

"Good, but so busy. It seems like forever since we've seen each other." Catherine smiled, her eyes lighting up, then she looked over at Barbara. She tugged on the ribbons of her prayer *kapp.* "From the look on Barbara's face, she didn't want to let you go. I know I shouldn't say this, and the Lord seeks for us to love everyone, but Barbara?" Catherine shook her head. "Sorry, but she's not the nicest person."

"Everyone has their flaws; we just have to accept them for who they are," Martha said.

Catherine patted Martha's arm. "You have a very kind heart, my friend."

They were deep into the conversation when Martha realized she had spent more than the five minutes given to her. She waved a goodbye to her friend and hurried past the stall, running to the parking lot.

"Oh no!" Martha cried. The buggy was gone! Barbara had kept to her warning of leaving her if she stayed too long. She let out a sigh. She wasn't going to let her stepmother's actions beat her down. She would walk home. After all, she had done it in the past. However, with the heavy basket she was carrying, it would take her longer than normal.

She had just taken a few steps when a buggy slowed down next to her. She continued walking, and the buggy stopped. She looked up, and her eyes widened in surprise.

It was him.

Isaiah, holding the reins of the horse, smiled at her. "Good afternoon, ma'am. Do you need a ride home? That basket looks quite heavy."

She stared up into his handsome face, unable to move. Her heart tripped as she tried to focus.

"Umm..." Her words seemed to evaporate from her mind, then she blinked. "If you don't mind, I would appreciate it."

To her surprise, he got down from the buggy, took her basket, then offered her his hand. She placed her hand in his as he helped her up into the buggy. His hand felt warm in hers, sending sparks up her spine. It shocked her so much, she quickly let go, and he returned to his seat.

"Thank you very much," Martha said, twisting the fabric of her skirt in her hands.

"I thought you came here with your stepmother. Where is she?" Isaiah asked, placing the basket on the floor of the buggy.

Her face turned red. How did he know she had come with Barbara? She looked at him, and he quickly looked away, his eyes on the road ahead.

"Umm… She left." Martha lowered her head.

"Why didn't you go home with her instead of walking back?"

Martha looked away, out into the fields. How could she answer him without lying to him?

"Well, you shouldn't walk home carrying such a heavy load. It's a long way for a young woman to be on the road alone. It's not safe," Isaiah said. He turned to her with a dazzling smile. "You know, Timothy is always talking about you, saying how good of a teacher you are."

Martha laughed jovially. That was so like Timothy to say. "Yes, he's rather fond of me, and the feeling is mutual. I'm very fond of him."

"If I must say, I think he has a crush on you," Isaiah said with a wink, which made her laugh once more.

"Oh, he's a sweet boy. He'll grow out of it. How do you like our community? Is it much different from the one you were raised in?" Martha asked.

"Well, as you know, all Amish communities are different with different rules. I loved my community in Wisconsin, but some things are done differently here. I'm sure I'll get used to it. This is home now, and I am glad to be here with my family," Isaiah said. "So far, I do find this community to be more relaxed. My former community was very strict. Sometimes the rules seemed to be too strict. For example, back home, we were not allowed to ride bicycles, but here it is allowed. I like it here."

"So, are you here to stay?" Martha asked.

Isaiah shrugged. "I believe so."

His answer made her happy, but she didn't know why. "Your father must be delighted," Martha said, silently adding that she was delighted as well.

Isaiah beamed with a fond smile at the mention of his father. "Yes, he's very much delighted. But not everyone's happy that I am here," he added with a downcast look.

"Don't worry about them. With time, they will realize that you have a good heart."

He gave her a long look. "And you know this how?"

Martha shrugged. "I just can tell. The Amish usually try to see the best in everyone. At least, they should."

Isaiah smiled. "Thanks. How is school going?"

Martha smiled happily. "Well, school was amazing today. Michael, one of my youngest students… I have no idea how he got a toad, but he hid it in Mirabel's desk. Timothy tried to get it out but only worsened the situation."

Isaiah doubled over in laughter as she told the story, tears at the corners of his eyes. "It must be fun every day."

Martha shook her head. "At times it is, but then at times, it can be really tiring dealing with children. They all want to be heard, and you need to listen to all of them at the same time. They get dirty, they play, and they make you laugh. But I love it a lot; being around children is refreshing. They don't judge others like adults. They are young at heart and innocent."

Martha grinned. "And every day is different. I love each one of the children."

"You really do love teaching," Isaiah said thoughtfully.

"I do… I love it a lot," Martha said. "I started teaching when I was sixteen when I was a teacher's assistant, following Miss Philip everywhere and learning the ropes."

"And you fell in love with it?"

"Yes, I did. It started out as a sanctuary for me. It was a way for me to leave home because I didn't want to be stuck at home all day. But I soon realized I loved it. I love the children, their laughs, their games. And I always feel sad when they finish school after the eighth grade."

"I hope Timothy is good in class." Isaiah smiled.

Martha giggled. "He's a curious kid, and he does get into trouble at times, but he's very well-mannered and kind."

"I'm glad you're passionate about teaching. It's beautiful to see someone else passionate about their dream," Isaiah said.

"And what's your dream?" Martha asked.

"I want to own my own carpentry business one day," he said. "For now, I am training under my father to be a carpenter. I would also like to be a minister or elder in the church someday. Since ministers and elders aren't paid here, we do need a trade, and I enjoy carpentry."

"That's an honourable decision," she said with admiration.

"Thank you. I love helping people by building and improving homes. I also love discussing God's word."

"I'm sure you'll excel at whatever you put your mind to."

"And you as well," he said with a smile.

She couldn't stop her cheeks from heating as she smiled back.

"Maybe you have heard about me being abandoned by my *Englisher* mother in the community I grew up in," Isaiah said with a hint of sadness.

She wished she could hug him and take away the sadness. "Well, I heard you grew up in an Amish community in Wisconsin, but I had no idea about your mother leaving you there. I'm so sorry."

Isaiah shrugged. "She didn't know what to do after giving birth to me because she couldn't take care of me emotionally or financially. She did what she thought was right."

"Were they good to you? I mean, those you grew up with?" Martha asked. Martha could relate. She put her stepmother in her prayers every night, hoping that the Lord would soon thaw her heart.

"I stayed with two families during my childhood. The first family I stayed with was a distant relation of my mother. They were... cruel to me. I grew up knowing that I was the odd one out, that I had been abandoned by my mother. Let's just say it was a sad part of my life."

"What changed?" Martha asked, her heart heavy for the young Isaiah who had grown up without his mother's love.

Isaiah smiled, his eyes brightening up. "I met Abram Daniels and his family. He was one of the elders in the community at the time. I was one of those naughty kids when I was younger." Isaiah grinned.

Martha giggled. She doubted that. He looked like he had been a gentleman when he had been a little boy. "Are you sure about that? You're well-mannered."

Isaiah laughed. "I learned to be. When I was younger, I was always causing mischief. I would run away from home and prank my classmates. My restlessness continued even in the church. That was how Minister Abram noticed me. I and a couple of other kids tried to frighten Margaret, his daughter, and she got a scrape on her knee. The others ran off, but I took her home."

"What did her father do?" Martha asked excited.

"Her mom, Angela, gave me the best meal I had ever had. Her father was kind to me. All of us sat down together, playing a game. It was the first time I had been a part of something so special. It was the first time I was part of a family, and even though I was eight, I knew I wanted more of it. So the next day, and then the next, I was at his home. It continued for a week, and then a month, and I had practically moved into their home. I even had a bed in their sons' room."

"And that was it?" Martha asked, knowing there was more to come.

He smiled at her impatience. "One night, I think about three months after that first night I spent with them, Abram and Angela sat me down after dinner and told me of their plans for me. They wanted to adopt me as a member of their family. I was surprised for a moment, then I began to cry. You see, I never knew I could get something so beautiful, and here they were offering it to me. I told them I wanted to be their son, and I left my old family and joined my new family. I am forever grateful to God that I met them. They instilled in me manners, kindness, and how to walk in the light of the Lord."

"Wow!" Martha wiped a tear from her eyes. His story had touched her greatly, showing how much the Lord was always in control. She was glad he had grown up with a beautiful family who had loved and cared for him.

"Living with Abram, seeing his kindness, his happiness, his love for people, the community, and the Lord... I was awed and drawn to the Lord. Abram is an amazing man whom I call father, and he made me love the word of the Lord and want to be a minister. He's my role model. He's not a perfect man, as he has his flaws, but we all have flaws, except for the Lord."

"Do you still talk to them?" Martha asked.

Isaiah nodded. "I do. I may be a part of this community, but they will always be in my heart. They were the ones who advised me to reach out to my father, and look what came out of it. I love them, and we still communicate with each other. My father has also met with them a few times, and he's grateful for their help in bringing me up in the way of the Lord."

"Your story is a reassurance of the Lord's love for us. He always cares for us, looking out for us." Martha added, "You will make a great carpenter." She could already see it in the kindness he emanated and how much he cared for others.

"Thank you. And you make a great teacher as well." Isaiah smiled.

She sighed, looking away. She knew she was a good teacher, but she couldn't help but think of what Jake had said to her. Jake was just one of the men who wouldn't want their wives to work outside the home. Here it was allowed for women to work outside the home, and many women worked at local bakeries, diners, or the farmers' market. And it was not only Jake who had disapproved of her teaching; her stepmother had done so as well, even though she'd spent some of the wages that Martha had given to her father.

Martha had also heard remarks from others, advising her to quit teaching when she got married.

"What is it?" Isaiah asked, noticing her sadness.

"I understand that according to the Amish way, the home is to be cared for and managed by the wife, but teaching is still my dream. I just wish I could teach forever, but I may get too busy with children of my own one day."

Isaiah smiled. "Your dream is very important to you. Your teaching is a gift given by God, and you shouldn't allow the opinion of others to weigh you down. You love it, and it is for the benefit of the community. When the time is right, when you face a dilemma about your dream, pray about it. The Lord always has a solution for our conflicts; you just have to seek his presence. And if you feel in your heart you should continue teaching for many years to come, then you should."

His words calmed her heart. He was right. She ought not to perturb herself with worries of the future. For now, she would continue to teach, and when she was conflicted, she would seek the Lord.

For the rest of the ride, Martha realized this was the deepest conversation she had had in a long time. He spoke about everything with passion and determination. She knew she was right in her impression of him. He was a kind-hearted person; she could see it from the simple things he did, like how he gently directed the horse pulling the buggy.

Martha's house came into view as the buggy approached it. Like the gentleman he was, he got down before her and helped her down. She told him not to bother, but he took the basket to the door before waving to her. She waved back to him fondly, wondering when she was going to see him next.

Her smile slipped when she opened the door. Standing in front of her was Barbara with a frown, hands on her hips. "Was that the lost son of Joseph Gray?" Barbara demanded.

"Yes, his name is Isaiah," Martha corrected.

"Hmm." Barbara's eyes followed Martha as she took the basket to the kitchen.

Martha said nothing about the incident in the market. She knew Barbara was waiting for her to bring it up so she could scold her, leading into a lengthy talk of how spoiled and disobedient she was. She wasn't going to fall into the trap her stepmother had set.

"You should know better than mingling with the likes of that boy," Barbara said, standing by the doorway.

She had known her stepmother would not let it be. "He's a very kind and helpful young man."

"He's a stranger and not welcome here," Barbara snapped.

"He is welcome here by everyone but you, it seems. Why is he not welcome by you? Because he wasn't brought up here? He's one of God's creations, isn't he? He plans to do the work of God, doesn't he? Then, he is surely one of us, and is welcome here," Martha replied coolly. Discrimination before God was not allowed, for everyone was equal; Barbara was being unfair by disliking a man who had done nothing wrong. He'd been born outside of the community, which had been beyond his control.

Barbara's eyes narrowed as she gave Martha a long look. "You like him, don't you?"

Martha shrugged. She wasn't going to deny it. The man was interesting and kind. "What's not to like?"

"Of course, your affections would be set on someone like that. Just remember you're promised to another."

Martha scoffed. "That's ridiculous. I am not promised to anyone."

"You must know Jake has wanted to marry you for a long time," Barbara said.

"And I have never agreed to marry him, much less even go on a date with him. I do not like Jake. There's something about him that makes me uncomfortable," Martha explained. "I've said that before."

"Here we go again with your excuses. How long do you want to continue to be a burden to your father and me?" Barbara asked with a glare.

Her words hurt Martha like an arrow shot to her heart. But she willed her tears not to fall, at least not in the presence of her stepmother. "I'm not a burden to my father."

Barbara stepped in front of her. "Do not complicate things. Jake is a good man who cares for you. I do not see what he sees in you, but you should consider yourself privileged to have him want you. Now, stop with all those excuses and agree to marry him."

Martha gave her stepmother a firm look. "No. I feel nothing for Jake, and I will not marry him."

Barbara laughed with scorn. "Well, we will see about that."

CHAPTER THREE

On Monday morning, once again, Martha was glad to be out of the house.

She was surprised that the time had flown by so quickly as the bell rang, signalling the end to the school day. She helped her students get ready for home, then she waved goodbye to them as they walked out. When she turned around, only little Timothy was left. She smiled as she ruffled his hair.

"Aren't you going home with the others, Timothy?" Martha asked.

Timothy shook his head. "No, ma'am. My big brother is coming to take me home. Have you seen my big brother?" Timothy asked with admiration in his eyes. "He's so big and tall. He's amazing. I have the best big brother!"

Martha laughed. It was obvious the little boy was glad to have a brother.

The sound of a buggy pulling up in front of the schoolroom made Timothy run outside. She heard his excited chatter as he talked to his brother.

She felt his presence the moment he entered the schoolroom. She looked up from her desk to his smiling face, which made most of her downcast thoughts disappear.

"Good afternoon, Martha," Isaiah said.

"Good afternoon." She grinned.

Timothy tugged at his brother's shirt, pulling him closer to Martha. "Miss Martha, this is my brother Isaiah. Isaiah, do you like her? She's very pretty, isn't she?" Timothy said, watching Isaiah expectantly.

Martha let out a giggle, her face turning red. The poor child had no idea how embarrassed she was. "We are not supposed to comment on outward appearances, Timothy. It's not the

Amish way. It's what's on the inside that matters."

Her face turned even more red when Isaiah said, "Yes, Timothy, she is very pretty."

A giggle spurted from Timothy's lips, relieving the awkwardness, and they all laughed.

"I apologize for his forwardness, but he's just being truthful," Isaiah said. "Even if we are not supposed to say it."

"Thank you," Martha said shyly, busying herself with stacking her books.

"Can we go home now?" Timothy bounced on his heels in excitement.

"Soon, Timothy. Do you need a ride home, Martha?" Isaiah caught himself.

"Thank you, but I still have some things to do here." Martha followed them out and waved to them as they left. She could have used that ride since she was tired, but she didn't need any scolding from Barbara. Besides, she had papers to grade before going home.

"Are you sure? We can wait," Isaiah offered.

"No, thank you. I may be a while. You go on home."

"We will see you later," Isaiah said, and Timothy waved goodbye as they left.

She went back to work.

Had they forgotten something? Martha heard the wheels of a buggy crunching gravel in the yard a few moments later. She was filled with dread as she saw it was Jake instead. She had avoided him for a week and had hoped it would continue.

"What was *he* doing here?" Jake demanded as he stormed into the room. He banged his hand on the desk, his face red with fury.

Martha jolted in shock, her eyes narrowed in confusion. "What are you talking about?"

"You know who I mean," Jake snapped.

"He came to get his brother."

"And that was why you are all smiles with him? You think I do not know this is not the first time you've seen each other?" Jake sneered.

Martha glowered. It was her turn to be angry. "Are you spying on me?"

"No. Of course not, but I have seen you around with him, and word travels fast. People say you are close."

She stood up with her arms folded across her chest, unwilling to hold back her anger. "I owe you no explanation for who I smile at or who I spend time with!"

Jake stepped back, surprised for a moment, then he laughed bitterly. "Yes, you do. We're going to get married, and you will do what I tell you to do. And if I say stay away from him, you will."

Martha shook her head vehemently. "Marry you? No, Jake, I am not getting married to you. I would never—"

A gasp escaped her as he strode forward and slapped her in the face.

She looked at him with widened eyes; he towered above her, his eyes glistening with evil intent, sending a chill all over her.

He let out a bitter laugh. "Don't be stupid, Martha. We're getting married. It doesn't matter how you feel. Don't ever think you can talk back to me. I am giving you lenience now, but once we get married, you will know your place." He reached for her and she flinched, moving away. "My father doesn't let my mother talk that way to him. He's a strict man, and actually, he prefers if we don't speak to him at all. But one thing I've learned from him is that I won't let you talk to me like that when we're married."

Martha had only actually spoken to Bill Sullivan a few times, as he mostly kept to himself. In fact, Martha would admit that she avoided him, only because she was intimidated by him. He had a cruel look in his eyes, and even when Martha tried to give him a kind smile, he'd only glower.

Was Bill Sullivan treating his family like Jake was treating her now? Is that where Jake had learned this? Martha wanted to ask him, but she couldn't find the words.

His eyes narrowed as if reading her thoughts, and she feared for a moment he would strike her again, but he stepped back and walked to the door.

He stopped and turned around, "This is my last warning. Stop seeing that abomination. He was not born Amish. His own mother didn't even want him, and his parents were not married. He has no place here, and he has no right to be around what belongs to me."

Martha collapsed in her chair the moment his buggy pulled away, still shocked by what had just happened.

The tears spilled out her eyes as the pain in her cheek throbbed. All because she had turned Jake down.

She had seen a side of him she had never seen before, and if his wife ever disobeyed him when married, more of that side would be revealed.

One thing was for sure—she would never be his wife.

Her father would believe her, but would people believe her if she told them what he'd done? He was liked by many in the community. He'd been so confident that he would have his way with her.

Well, she knew *Daed* would believe her and support her. Now she just had to find the right time to tell him when she could get him alone.

She didn't want to talk to him about it with her stepmother around.

A man like Jake, so confident in his evil ways, was a man to be deeply concerned about.

CHAPTER FOUR

All through dinner, Martha was quiet. She barely listened to the conversation over the food. All she could think of was what had happened earlier in the day.

Her attention perked up when she heard Isaiah's name mentioned.

"What did you say?" Martha asked.

"I was just telling your mother that Isaiah is training to be a carpenter," *Daed* said. "And he wants to also become a minister or church elder one day."

"He's a stranger, remember? Who knows what changes he's going to bring? I tell you, that boy is up to no good; I see the trouble in his eyes," Barbara admonished.

Her father was quiet for a moment as he contemplated what his wife had said. "Yes, he is new to town, but the Bible says to love our neighbors," *Daed* said.

Martha could see what her stepmother was trying to do. She was trying to influence her father to think wrongly of Isaiah. It wasn't fair. All because she liked Jake, she was trying to cause strife for a man who didn't deserve it.

She now knew why Jake didn't like Isaiah. He must see the competition Isaiah brought with his arrival to the community.

Just as she was about to leave for her room, *Daed* called her back, patting the side of the wooden chair for her to sit.

"How is school?" her father asked.

"Things are going fairly well," Martha said.

There was a moment of silence then *Daed* said, "Jake paid me a visit today."

Her heart dropped at Jake's name. "What did he want?" she asked as she played with a thread sticking out of her dress.

"I'm sure you already know of his feelings for you, but since you have failed to inform me of your intention to get married, he decided to do so. I'm very glad he told me. I believe it is about time," her father continued.

Martha's eyes widened in dismay. She shook her head defiantly. "*Daed,* I don't want to marry him!"

His face frowned in confusion. "But he said you agreed to. Why did he say that?"

A bitter laugh spurted out of her. "Did he also tell you that he struck me? He slapped me in the face when I told him I would not marry him."

"What?" *Daed* asked in surprise, standing up. "How dare he?" he asked, his face reddened.

"Yes, he hit me today in the schoolroom because I told him I would not marry him!"

Martha cried. "He is lying about us being engaged. I don't ever want to see him again."

Her father threw his hands in the air. "I'm shocked. And here he was, lying right to my face, telling me how he cared for you. All this time, he's acted so kind. At least we know his true personality now rather than later."

"I won't marry Jake. People should know he is violent," Martha said.

"Of course, you won't marry him. I don't even want you near him." *Daed's* hands balled up into fists as he settled back onto his chair. He'd always been a devoted follower of the *Ordnung,* which was completely against violence, but right now he looked as if he wanted to pummel Jake Sullivan.

She should have foreseen Jake would create a web of deceit. He was even a more horrible person than she had thought. "I have never supported his advances towards me," Martha said. "I would never marry him. I never will. I don't trust him."

Barabara listened, her eyes wide in disbelief. Martha couldn't tell if she believed her side of the story or not.

Daed stood up. "I need to pray about this. We will speak to the elders about Jake's behavior. What he did was horribly wrong, and he is a danger to this community." He turned to her, his eyes soft. He touched her cheek, then stood again and pulled her into a hug. "I am so sorry this happened to you, my daughter. I will do my best to make this right."

"Thank you, *Daed.*" Martha wiped away a tear, grateful for her father's support.

"Now, I must pray for wisdom on how to handle this situation. I will speak to the elders tomorrow. Get some rest, my dear." Her father patted her arm and went up to his room.

Barbara shook her head as her sons sat with surprised expressions.

"I can't believe Jake did that," Neil said, and Richard nodded in agreement.

"He didn't," Barbara said. "How dare you spread lies about Jake, Martha."

"What?" Martha said, baffled. "But it's the truth."

"Jake would never do such a thing. You should go to your room and pray about what you've done. I won't tell your father you lied, but you should when you finally decide to tell the truth."

"I am telling the truth, and you will see that soon enough. The truth always comes to light." Martha went up to her room, distraught. How could her own stepmother not believe her?

She closed her eyes and mumbled a prayer, sitting on her bed. *God, please help me. Please take this burden away from me. A marriage ought to be a blissful union between a man and a woman. You know I have done nothing wrong, you know I have never led him on in any way. Please, take this burden away from me and bring happiness to me. Amen.*

When she opened her eyes, she felt the burden removed from her shoulders. She smiled amidst her tears. She was convinced everything would be all right. God was in total control.

***

Martha woke up the next day with a heavy heart. She knew God was in control, but she wondered what she could do to get Jake to stay away from her. He had not been joking when he told her they were going to get married, with or without her consent, but she couldn't let that happen.

She found herself slipping in and out of her thoughts while she taught the children at school. Today was one of those days she wanted all to herself to think. A thought occurred to her, one which upset her.

Should she leave the community? The thought was quickly shelved. No, she would not leave. She would remain here and fight her way out of this mess. Besides, she loved it here, and this was her home. She'd always dreamed of living here forever.

When she saw Isaiah's buggy stop in front of the schoolroom, her heart raced excitedly. At least, a ray of hope in this trying time. However, she reminded herself of the trouble caused by speaking with him.

She scolded herself. She would not obey Jake just to boost his ego.

"Hello, Martha," Isaiah greeted her.

"Hello," she said, consumed with sadness.

"Are you okay?" Isaiah asked.

Martha sighed. "Well, some things have happened that are weighing on my mind."

"Do not let the world weigh you down. You're a conqueror through Christ who strengthens you," Isaiah advised.

His words warmed her heart. He was right; she was a conqueror. "Thank you for your kind words."

They both looked to the door as Jake appeared. His eyes shot with anger at the sight of them. Martha took a step back, as if anticipating a hit from where she stood.

"Isaiah," Jake said with a smile. "How are you?"

"Jake," Isaiah said. "I'm well. And you?"

"Good. I see that you're here with my fiancée," Jake said.

Surprise dwelled on Isaiah's face, and he turned to Martha for confirmation.

"We're not getting married, Jake! Stop being deluded, and stop lying!" Martha spat in anger. "You lied to my father. Now stop lying about us getting married."

Jake took a step forward, and she knew if Isaiah was not present, he would have struck her again. Instead, he let out a laugh. "Oh, Martha. The things you say sometimes. Isn't she a funny one?"

Isaiah just stared at him, confused. He glanced at Martha, pain in his expression. Did he really believe Jake over her? "I should be going, I will see you later, Martha."

Martha wanted to tell him not to go, but felt paralyzed by fear that it would upset Jake even more. What should she say or do? Before she could decide, Isaiah was walking away.

Jake kept quiet until Isaiah walked out. Then Jake turned to Martha. She stepped back when she saw the hatred in his eyes. "How dare you talk back to me. Don't you remember what I said about that? And he calls you by your first name?" Jake sneered.

"Everyone calls me—"

She did not see the blow coming to her face. It knocked her off her balance, making her stumble and scream as she fell to the floor. She held her face in surprise. He leapt towards her, and before she could step away from him, he had pounced on her. He stifled her scream with his hand placed over her mouth. His hands encircled her neck, his grip tightening and cutting off her air supply more and more with each second.

"I have warned you not to talk to that outsider again. Haven't I?" He let out a mean laugh. "Do you like him? Of course, you like that scoundrel."

She felt the whole world disappearing around her as her vision tunnelled from lack of oxygen. Was this how she would die? She tried to kick and hit him, but the effort only exhausted her.

Jake finally let go of her, then she faintly heard voices and a squabble. Her eyes blinked open and closed as she tried to gain her senses of all that was happening. When she did, she saw Jake and Isaiah exchanging blows.

He came back for her.

Her eyes closed, and everything went dark.

***

When she opened her eyes, she was staring into Isaiah's face. There were a few bruises on his face, but he had a smile for her. "Are you okay?" he asked with concern.

"What... What happened?" Martha stammered. She tried to sit up, but a sharp pain filled her head.

She realized she was on a bed and looked around. She was in a strange room. She looked to Isaiah.

"I brought you to my family's home. It's closer than your house," Isaiah said.

"Thank you," Martha said. He had done the right thing by bringing her here instead. "What happened?" she asked.

"Call it my instincts, but I decided to come back to the schoolhouse to make sure you were safe, then I heard you scream, and I saw him hurting you. I should never have left; none of this would have happened," Isaiah said.

"But now you know how he truly is," she murmured. "It's not your fault, Isaiah. Jake... He's a bitter person. You shouldn't have gotten into a fight with him," Martha said. She had a feeling Jake would try to get back at him.

Isaiah sighed. "I know the Lord doesn't want us to use violence and fight with each other, but Jake could have hurt you much worse if I hadn't tried to stop him. I had to intervene, and me telling him to stop didn't work." He shook his head. "He was clearly lying about you getting married."

"Yes, he's lying. We are not getting married. I would never marry that selfish, arrogant man. Yesterday I told him I didn't want to marry him and he slapped me in the face. Then, today, after you walked out, he hit me again and tried to choke me because I was talking to you. He's extremely controlling, manipulative, and he's violent."

Isaiah just listened to her, and he wrapped his arm around her shoulders.

Martha continued, "I don't know why he thinks we are getting married. I've never even flirted with him. Honestly, I can't stand him, and I hate being around him. I told my father what happened yesterday, and he's going to speak to the elders about it. And now things have gotten even worse since then. I just feel trapped. I'm worried that the worst thing that'll happen to him is that he'll be shunned."

It felt so good to offload all she had been going through in the past weeks to someone else. Isaiah listened quietly, and if not for the way his eyes flashed, she would never have been able to tell that he was angry, but only reining it in.

"How can he treat you like this? Women should be respected. He's just a big bully," Isaiah spat. He paced the room. "I had a feeling there was more to him than meets the eye. I could feel the hostility underneath his smile. He's one of those people who has made my stay here unwelcome. I pondered what I had done to warrant such treatment, but I realized it was not of my own doing, but just his mean nature." Isaiah sighed and sat on the bed. "You shouldn't go through this alone. You shouldn't let him get away with his actions. We have to do something. I want to help you through this."

Martha sighed, smiling at him in relief.

"I'll do whatever I can," he said. "And I promise this. If you don't want to marry him, I will make sure that will never happen."

There was a knock on the door, and Ruth, Isaiah's stepmother, walked through the open door. Concern filled her eyes at the injuries all over Isaiah and Martha's faces, then she hugged Martha. "I'm so sorry for this," Ruth apologized.

"Thank you," Martha said. The only one at fault was Jake, who had chosen to be a bully instead of accepting the rejection.

"I hope that now people will know how he truly is so he won't ever hurt another woman again," Martha said.

"Exactly," Isaiah said. "This needs to end now. Maybe at least that one good thing will come of this."

Martha glanced at the clock on the wall and realized she must have been away from home for hours. They must be worried about her. "I should go home. My family must be worried about me," Martha said, trying to get up.

"I will take you home," Isaiah said, helping her up.

The buggy ride home was quiet. There was a blast of cold air, and Martha huddled into her coat. Her body ached from the hard fall on the floor, and her face ached from where she'd been struck. She had no idea how she looked, but it had to be horrible. There was no way she could go to the schoolhouse tomorrow looking and feeling like this.

The darkness had almost descended when they arrived. Isaiah helped her out of the buggy, and she leaned on him as he guided her to the house. The door was instantly thrown open, and her father stood at the doorway. Martha tried to read his face.

"What's going on? What has happened?" *Daed* asked. "Because Jake was just here and said some disconcerting things."

"What things?" Martha asked.

"Jake stopped by, and he told us all that happened," Barbara said from behind Martha's father.

"Now, Barbara, we don't even know if he was telling the truth or not. He has lied before. Let's see what Martha and Isaiah have to say about it."

Martha sighed. Would she never be free from Jake and his mean antics?

"Things are probably not as they were told. Please let us explain," Isaiah said.

Her father opened the door and let them inside, and he gasped as she came into the light, her injuries coming into view. Even Barbara's eyes widened in surprise as she clutched her chest.

"What happened?" her father asked.

Martha said quickly, "It was Jake. He attacked me."

"Jake? Of course not! There's no way he would have done such a thing," Barbara said.

"Well, he did. When I pulled him away from her, she was going unconscious. If I hadn't stopped him, he could have seriously injured or even killed her," Isaiah said.

"He told us he saw the both of you in an uncompromising position, and you hurt him to stop him from talking," *Daed* said. "He said Martha got caught in the middle, trying to break up the fight, and got hurt that way. Obviously, he was lying. I didn't believe him for a second."

Barbara shook her head slowly, rolling her eyes.

"He's lying. I admire your daughter, and I would never hurt or dishonor her," Isaiah said.

"When I came into the room, Jake was choking Martha. I yelled at him to stop, and he ignored me, so I pulled him off her and he punched me, so we got into a fight. I was just trying to stop him. I know the community does not condone violence, but I am afraid he may have seriously hurt her or worse if I had not intervened."

Martha's heart swelled with his confession, her heart racing. She closed her eyes and instantly opened them as a shudder ran through her.

Her father sighed when Isaiah was done. "I believe you."

"Do you really think Jake would lie about this?" Barbara asked.

Martha's father flashed his wife a look, silencing her instantly, then turned to Isaiah. "There have been a few whispers of Jake being violent, but they have been overlooked in the past. But I believe you, Isaiah. You're a good man, and I believe my daughter. She clearly trusts you and not Jake."

Martha nodded.

"She's an honorable, honest woman. Thank you for saving my daughter. It fills me with fear to think of what could have happened if you hadn't been there," *Daed* continued.

"I'm glad I was there too. So, what happens now?" Isaiah asked.

"I will speak to the elders again. I did earlier today, but nothing had been decided yet, and I will also tell them about this. They have to be made aware of what has happened," *Daed* said firmly.

"Agreed. I should go," Isaiah said to Martha. "I'll let you have time with your family. Please take care. Get some rest."

"Thank you very much," Martha said.

He gave her a kind smile, and her father saw him out. It seemed like Barbara had something to say, but she kept her lips pursed in dissatisfaction.

When her father returned, he hugged Martha, and she wept on his shoulder. It felt so good to be in his arms. She missed the father she once had, and how happy he had been before her mother died. But tonight, he had defended her and believed her, and she was grateful.

"Everything will be all right," *Daed* reassured her.

Martha knew her father was right—everything was going to be fine. Her prayers had been answered; even if she had to go through pain for it, she was free from living a life of misery.

CHAPTER FIVE

Two weeks had gone by and Martha had spent the time recovering. The injuries had left visible wounds, and it would take some time for them to fade away. However, the mental and emotional wounds would take longer to heal.

She still had nightmares, but she prayed every night, and they were occurring less frequently. She had not been able to go to school because she had no explanation to give the children for her bruises that would not upset them, and her father had told her to take some time off. A substitute had been filling in for her.

Today she returned to the schoolroom, and she was glad to see the smiles on the children's faces. They swarmed around her, excited about her return.

"We're glad to have you back, Miss Martha. We heard you got hurt," Timothy said with concern glistening in his eyes on behalf of the other children.

She ruffled his hair playfully. She was glad to be back too. The excuse given for her absence had been because of an injury, but news travelled fast in the community, and there was no doubt most of them knew what had transpired between Jake and her.

A few days after the attack, the elders had paid her a visit to listen to her story of what Jake had done. She recalled the look of dismay on their faces when they saw the wounds and hand marks on her neck.

Jake had been called to a gathering of the elders, with Martha's father present. He had denied the accusations against him, calling them merely lies and made up stories. As Jake had told Martha's father, he said he had found Isaiah and Martha in a sinful position and had been beaten up by Isaiah. He said Martha had been caught in the middle of the scuffle, trying to stop them. Isaiah had denied all the accusations.

After going over each person's story and seeing Martha's injuries, the elders decided that Jake would be shunned by the entire community. No one could speak to him or do business with him, or they would be shunned as well. This would continue until Jake repented and asked the community for forgiveness, but Jake was too smug to repent for the time being. He was also directed by the elders to stay away from Martha and the schoolhouse.

It was the Amish way not to report crimes to the police, so nothing else would be done to punish Jake. But she knew the Lord was a God of justice and he would fight for her.

And now at least all the women in the community knew to stay away from him.

At least, with all that happened, she was not going to get married to Jake. That was the only good thing that had come out of this incident. He would get his punishment from God when the time was right. She was sure of it. It was only a matter of time before he made another mistake and slipped; then his evil ways would be made known for all to be aware of.

He had the opportunity to repent, but if he didn't, he would face the wrath of the Lord. Had she forgiven him? No, it would take some time to forgive him, but she would move on from the horrible incident.

***

After school ended for the day, Martha waited patiently with Timothy for his older brother. In these trying times, Isaiah was the rock who stood by her. He picked her up along with Timothy after school each day, and had even come to her house to sit with her and make sure she was doing well. They had spent some time talking about themselves and the community, and they'd even played games together and with Timothy.

Isaiah was truly an insightful person. She could see in him a great minster who would lead the people down the right path.

Timothy jumped in excitement and ran to greet his brother as the buggy arrived in front of the school. Martha was also excited as she walked out front to greet Isaiah.

"How are you, Martha?" Isaiah asked.

"I'm doing much better," Martha said.

"Do you mind if I take you home again?" he asked.

"I would love it if you would," Martha said.

They laughed amidst Timothy's excited chattering as Isaiah took her home. When he asked if he could stop by later in the evening to take her for a ride in his buggy, she knew her day had been made complete. Her answer was yes, and she waltzed into the house with a smile. It dropped when she saw Barbara with a disapproving look.

"Do you know what they are saying about you?" Barbara asked.

"What are they saying?" Martha asked.

"They are calling you an unchaste woman," Barbara said, shaking her head. "I did warn you, to be content with what you had. Trust me, it will be a surprise if you ever marry."

Martha's blood ran cold as her heart plummeted. There was only one person who could spread such rumors about her. Would Jake not stop being a menace to her? Wouldn't he accept his loss and move on?

"This isn't fair that after what he has done, he still gets to spread malicious lies about me," Martha said sadly.

"You know, something similar happened to me once, except the rumors were true. I'm sorry if I'm hard on you, but I'm just trying to help you. I don't want you to end up like me," Barbara told her.

"Like you? What do you mean? You have a good life," Martha said in surprise.

"My life wasn't always this way. I'm blessed your father wanted to marry me even with what happened in my past." Barbara's blue eyes lowered.

"What do you mean? What happened?" Martha immediately flinched, wondering if she'd asked too much. "Sorry. You don't have to answer that."

"Let's just say I made some bad choices. I was blessed and got a second chance. So I just don't want you to make bad choices like I did."

Barbara walked away, clearly not wanting to talk about it anymore, but Martha's mind reeled.

What had Barbara done, and what had happened before she'd met Martha's father?

***

Isaiah picked up Martha in his buggy, and they stopped by the pond to talk. Martha was glad for the peace and quiet. She loved her family and her students, but sometimes she just needed to hear herself think.

"Do not worry about what people say. In time, they will learn to understand that you're an amazing person and that those rumors are false. Also, know that you have lots of people who care about you," Isaiah said, and Martha gave him a questioning look. "I can tell it's on your mind."

Martha sighed. "You're right. It's been on my mind a lot. I'm trying not to worry, because God commands us not to worry, but it's so hard not to. Besides, in the past few days, I've received visitors from the community who have come to show their support and that they don't believe the rumors, so I'm thankful for that."

Isaiah patted her hand. "It's going to be all right."

Martha nodded.

"So, I do have some good news. I spoke to your father, and I asked him for permission to court you with the intention of marriage. He gave us his blessing, and now I would like to ask you something. Would you like to be my girlfriend?" Isaiah asked, a wide grin on his face.

"Yes!" Martha threw her arms around him and hugged him, joy filling her. Finally, some good news. "I'm so happy. It feels like this is the one good thing that has happened in a long time."

"I was quite nervous to talk to your father, I'll admit. He's intimidating. But it's only because he loves you so much, and now especially after everything that has happened, he's more protective of you than ever. I promised him I'd take good care of you no matter what. I guess he trusts me."

"Of course, he trusts you."

"Well, I would have understood if he didn't trust any man with his daughter after what happened."

"You're not any man, though." Martha smiled up at him and squeezed his hand.

Comfortable silence descended on them as they sat by the pond, both of them lost in contented thoughts. Conversation soon picked up, and they talked for hours. It was refreshing for Martha. She had few friends, and even then, she rarely got to spend time with them. Isaiah was a conversationalist, filled with positivity that flowed to her. He was an amazing person, and she admired him even more.

"It's getting dark. I should take you home," Isaiah said, staring at the sky.

She was sad to go, wishing the night would never end, but it was the right thing to do.

The buggy stopped in front of the house. He helped her out, following her to the front door.

"May I see you tomorrow after school? If you're free, that is," Isaiah asked politely.

"Yes, you may," Martha said happily. She waved to him before going inside. She was not surprised to see Barbara drop the curtain from where she had been watching, a look of disapproval on her face.

Martha went inside to see Barbara standing in the entryway.

"You're shameless, aren't you? The whole community is buzzing with what you have gotten yourself involved in, and yet you're frolicking around with another man. You ought to be gloomy and thinking about your now meager prospects of getting married," Barbara said with a sneer.

"Thank you for caring," Martha said with a forced smile. "But Isaiah already spoke with

Daed, and he gave us his blessing to court. So, we've done nothing wrong."

With that, Martha walked up to her room, leaving Barbara standing there, scowling.

There was no use trying to get Barbara to see things the right way; it would result in her hurting her even more. What she had with Isaiah was a wonderful relationship, one she was grateful for.

She had put it in her prayers, and she knew everything would work out for the best.

CHAPTER SIX

It was one of those days that had started out wrong. Distracted, she'd burned breakfast, and she had to hurry off to school on an empty stomach.

At school, it seemed as though a memo had been passed amongst the children to be extra naughty.

Even Timothy, who was usually well behaved, had a few tricks up his sleeve. She just couldn't wait for the school day to be over. What she was looking for at the end of the day was her usual buggy ride with Isaiah. Hopefully, that would take the strain of the day away.

They had fallen into a routine over the past several months. After school, he either took her home or picked her up from the house, and they would spend time together with each other's families. At times, he had dinner with her family. *Daed* liked Isaiah, but Barbara remained cold to him, as she was with Martha. She also often had dinner with his family too, and they were all warm and friendly.

The more time she spent with Isaiah, the more she realized that she was falling deeply in love with him. He had become a confidant, someone she could share her thoughts with and someone who always supported her.

When school was over that day, she packed her things into her bag, looking out for Isaiah's buggy.

"Are you not waiting for your brother?" she asked Timothy as he joined the other children who were walking home.

Timothy slapped his forehead as he remembered a message he had been given to deliver. "Oh, Miss Martha. My brother told me he would not be able to see you today. He had to go off with our father out of town."

"Oh!" Her heart fell at Timothy's message. She had truly been looking forward to seeing him. "Do you know when they are getting back?"

"No." He shook his head as his friends called out to him. He looked at her with excited eyes, ready to join his friends. She waved him goodbye.

Going back home was a slow walk. Martha had hoped seeing Isaiah would make her day better. She smiled as she shook the sadness away. When he returned, they would make up for his absence.

The next day, she headed to the market with the buggy and a shopping list. She was glad to go alone, eager to get some time away from Barbara, who would push her all around the market. At least she'd have some time to catch up with her friends without being told to hurry about or miss her ride home.

Her friends squealed in excitement like they usually did when they saw her. Giggling, Martha hurried over to them.

"How have you been, Martha?" Catherine asked.

"Good," Martha replied.

"Where's Isaiah?" Antonia asked, looking behind her.

She had introduced Isaiah to them at church, and she could tell they liked him. Like her, they were glad that Jake was out of her life.

"He went out of town with his father," Martha said.

"I know you miss him already." Catherine smiled.

"I do not," Martha said.

"You do," Antonia said.

"I do not," Martha pushed on with a smile.

The three of them burst into a laugh with Martha shaking her head, amused. She sure had missed seeing her friends outside of church. They talked some more as she bought what the house needed, and afterwards, she waved to them, hoping to see them in a few days at church.

A smile was on her face as she carried the items to her buggy, prepared to start the trip back home. The smile slipped away when she saw who was standing by her buggy.

Since the incident involving Jake, she had only seen him from a distance, choosing to ignore him. Thankfully, their paths barely crossed, and the only time they were in the same place was at public gatherings—until now.

At the sight of him, her heart raced. Not the way she did when she saw Isaiah—her heart rate always increased with excitement and joy. But when she saw Jake, her heart pounded with fear.

Ignoring him and trying to hide her unease, she placed the bags in the buggy. She had no idea what he was doing here. She hoped she hid her nervousness well enough.

As she tried to get in the buggy, he stood in her way. Looking up at him with a scowl, Martha said, "You're shunned. You know I can't speak to you. Go away."

Jake cackled, sending a chill down her spine. "You have a sharp mouth now, don't you?" he sneered. "Besides, I already repented to the elders. I'm not shunned anymore. So yes, you can talk to me now."

Martha felt the blood drain from her face. No, it couldn't be. Just like that, he'd "repented"? He had to have been lying, and the elders had lifted the shunning all because of his fake repentance?

Even just looking at him now, Martha could see how obvious it was that Jake didn't think he'd done anything wrong. But he'd probably put on a magnificent performance for the elders, and they'd been convinced that his repentance had been heartfelt.

"Oh, yes. Everything is fine now. I'm back in the fold, where I belong. And now I can talk to you again," he said smugly.

"What do you want?" Martha repeated.

"I just wanted to see how miserable you are without me in your life," Jake said.

Martha laughed humourlessly. Who did he think he was? Her life had gotten better since the incident. She had a more supportive family as well as friends, and she had Isaiah in her life. "I'm courting Isaiah. Haven't you heard? You really do have a high opinion of yourself, don't you?" Martha asked.

Jake's eyes narrowed. "You think you're better than me, huh? I have seen you going around with that man. You know he has nothing to offer you. He's an outcast. He's just going to use and dump you. You're scorned, but he will make you an outcast as well."

"Thank you for your concern," Martha said. "But Isaiah is twice the man you'll ever be. You're a thoughtless jerk who actually would use and abuse me, as you already have, and I would rather die than ever be with you." He'd only come to rattle and manipulate her. She knew him better after what he had done to her. The only person he was concerned about was himself. "Kindly excuse me so I can go home," Martha said, tired of him and his intrusion as she tried to walk past him to the buggy.

Anger shone in his eyes as he glared at her. Before, she would have fidgeted from him, her gaze lowered, but not this time. She looked up at him, her gaze not wavering from his. They held each other's gaze, and although her eyes stung, she refused to look away. He scowled as he finally looked away, and a victorious smile spread on her lips. However, her joy was short-lived.

"I do pity you. You should count yourself lucky that I ever wanted to have you for a wife. Rest assured, I was the best thing to ever happen to you. Your fate is miserable; you will end up a lonely old maid," Jake spat.

She laughed again. "Yeah, sure. And so what if I did end up single? There's nothing wrong with that. I would be content, and I'd rather be single my entire life than marry someone like you."

She had heard enough of his attempts to demean her. She tried to walk away to the other side of the buggy, but his hand gripped around her wrist. With hot anger and indignation, Martha turned to him, waving a finger in his face.

She was usually not an angry person. Perhaps it was the thought of how he had hurt her in the past. Perhaps it was the thought of how he had tried to manipulate her to marry him, or it might have been his cruel words that had gotten to her.

"Don't ever come near me again, Jake. You may have gotten away with it when you hurt me, but the next time you try to do so again, the Lord will fight for me, and you will get the punishment you deserve!" she shouted with a voice that sounded stronger than she felt, which drew the attention of everyone nearby. "Now let go of me!"

People in the parking lot were now watching, looking concerned.

Jake's eyes widened as he stared at her in shock.

"Hey! Get away from her!" Catherine and Antonia called, rushing out of the store.

Jake looked up at them, then released his hold on her, glowering. Martha glared at him as he walked away and climbed into his buggy. She could feel his gaze on her as his buggy drove off, heart racing in excitement and disbelief at what had happened.

Martha had always been a people pleaser, always polite and afraid to hurt anyone's feelings. She'd never stood up for herself like that in her life, and it felt amazing—so empowering.

At that moment, she felt as though she could conquer anything.

"We just looked out the window and saw Jake grabbing your wrist. What happened? Did he hurt you?" Antonia asked.

She and Catherine both wrapped their arms around Martha.

"Oh my, you're shaking," Catherine said. "Are you okay?"

Martha let out a calming breath. "Actually, I'm great. I can't believe it, but I just stood up to that pompous bully. He didn't hurt me, but he tried to talk down to me. I didn't let him get to me."

"Good. He's the worst." Antonia wrinkled her nose.

"I was ready to come out here and punch his lights out," Catherine added hotly.

"Catherine! You know that is not the Amish way," Antonia said. "The Amish don't condone violence."

Catherine shook her head. "Sometimes I don't agree with that. If I saw that guy hit you again, I don't know if I could stop myself. Take that. And that!" Catherine punched the air dramatically.

The girls laughed at Catherine's joke, and Martha felt the tension and fear start to slip away.

"I love you two. Thanks so much for looking out for me," she said.

"Of course. That's what best friends are for," Antonia said.

Martha said goodbye and got in her buggy, then went on her way. She stopped the buggy in the corner of the road to take a deep breath and compose herself. Her heart still raced, and her eyes closed as she calmed herself. What would Isaiah do if he was here? He would remind her to pray, and this she did.

Thank you, Lord, for seeing me through. Thank you for helping me stand up against Jake. Thank you for protecting me and giving me courage. I feel it in my heart that this is the last time he will ever disturb me, now that he knows I will always stand up to him. I believe I am free of him at last. Thank you, Lord.

She felt much better as she continued the ride home. Her stepbrothers ran out to meet her to bring the groceries into the house. *Daed* wasn't home. He had gone to visit a few families and would be back by dinner. Barbara sat in the living room with a ball of yarn on her lap while she knitted.

She looked up at Martha's entry, and Martha's composure fell when she saw the look on her stepmother's face. It was not a good one; it seemed to bear bad news.

"Thank you, Neil and Richard, for bringing in the groceries. That was so kind of you," Barbara said, eyeing Martha. "Now, Martha, come sit with me."

With a look of resignation, Martha sat beside her stepmother. Humming quietly, Barbara said nothing, the knitting pin going in and out of the scarf she was working on. Finally, just as Martha was about to excuse herself, Barbara said, "How long will you continue to frolic around with that young man? That Isaiah. The scorn you have brought to this family... Isn't it enough? Will you be satisfied when you have tarnished our names completely?"

"Well, since I intend to marry him, I'll be spending a lot of time with him. I have done nothing wrong," Martha said. "I told you, we are courting with the intention of marriage. I don't understand why you dislike him so much. He's such a kind man."

"Well, I heard he's not going to marry you. There are rumors..."

Martha paled. "Rumors?"

Barbara nodded. "Yes, rumors that he's seeking another young lady's hand in marriage, and just dating and running around with you for fun. What will become of you? You will remain an old maid who will stay in her father's house always."

"That can't be true. Isaiah and I plan on getting married," Martha argued. What was Barbara talking about?

"Keep telling yourself that. Just do not bring more shame to this family. We have had enough scandal already. It is sad that you will never marry because no one will have you," Barbara said with a look of dismissal.

Martha shot up out of her seat, her hands in fists. "Why do you dislike me so much? Have I done something to offend you?" Martha asked, the words spilling out before she could stop them.

Barbara hesitated, setting the yarn and knitting needles on her lap. "I don't dislike you. It's just that...you remind me of someone. Also, I don't want you to make the same bad choices I made when I was your age. I'm sorry if I seem harsh, but I really am trying to help you. So, listen to me when I say you should avoid that Isaiah or you might bring shame on this family."

Martha hesitated. What was Barbara not telling her?

"Now go on up to your room," Barbara urged.

Martha pivoted on her heel and marched away. Tears filled Martha's eyes as she went to her room and sat on her bed. Barbara's words had filled her with sadness. She'd done nothing indecent with anyone. She knew God was in control of everything. Who was her stepmother to declare that she would never be married and have a happy family, all because she didn't want her to make the same bad choices as her? Martha was not like Barbara at all, and never would be.

She was half asleep when she heard Isaiah's voice at the front door. She sat up.

"She's not around," she heard Barbara say to Isaiah. "She doesn't want to see you."

Suddenly, Martha sprang up from the bed and hurried out of the room. The door had already closed and, ignoring Barbara's warning look, she ran after Isaiah before he could get on the buggy.

"Isaiah!" she called.

He turned around, surprised. "Your stepmother said you didn't want to see me."

Martha said dryly, "She lied."

Isaiah hesitated, obviously at a loss for words. After a moment he said, "Would you like to go for a ride?"

She nodded. He took her hand in his, helping her in to the buggy.

"Something terrible has happened. I saw Jake at a store in town, and he told me he repented before the elders and the shunning has been lifted. He's not going anywhere," Martha explained, looking away with a heavy heart.

"What? How did this happen? Wait, are you okay? What did he do to you?"

"He just grabbed my arm and tried to talk down to me, but I didn't let him. I told him to let me go and leave me alone and that God would punish him. Then Catherine and Antonia ran out of the store, and he left. I have a feeling he won't be bothering me anymore. I really stood my ground, and it felt great."

"Well, I'm glad he didn't hurt you. I don't know what I would have done if he had hurt you again. And I'm glad you stood up for yourself. Maybe now he's seen that you're not afraid of him, he really will leave you alone. I will pray for that."

"Thanks. I do believe in my heart that God will give him what he deserves."

"I think so, too. Listen, I apologize for not telling you I was leaving for a trip out of town. It was impromptu," Isaiah apologized. "We were helping a friend move."

"It's okay." Martha flashed a smile.

She remained silent as he talked about his trip; she was lost in her thoughts, remembering what her stepmother had said to her.

Isaiah stopped the buggy at the pond, their usual spot. The twilight twinkled on the black water, mirroring the sky. A gentle breeze blew, and Martha wrapped the blanket Isaiah had given her more tightly around her.

"Martha," Isaiah said.

She looked up at him. "Yes?"

"Tell me please, what's wrong? Did something else happen?" Isaiah asked, his voice laded with concern.

"It's…" She paused for a moment, then she told him all that had happened with her stepmother. She told him of the hurtful words Barbara had told her. "I just… I feel sad and hurt hearing such words from her. I hope someday she will learn to care for me like she does for her sons. A part of me wonders if she said those words out of spite or if they are indeed right. She hinted that something happened to her in her past, that she'd made bad choices. But I don't know why she said those things."

Isaiah patted her hand. "I'm sorry about what your stepmother said. I understand how much words can hurt a person. Growing up, it wasn't easy for me either, and I am grateful to God that he showered me with love. Do not worry about your stepmother's fears. She's not God, who is our Creator. She cannot decide if you will be happy or not."

"Listen. My stepmother told me something quite disturbing. She said you plan on marrying another woman and are only dating me for fun."

Isaiah laughed. "There are indeed no secrets in this small community. The person who started that rumor must have overheard me talking to my father, and they must not have waited to hear the end of the discussion. That woman I plan on marrying is you. I'm not courting anyone else. I was talking to my father outside the church. Any single man should consider himself blessed by the Lord to have you as a wife. I guess I should have spoken with him somewhere more private."

She was speechless as she gazed up at him. Had he just said those words or had she heard wrong? A smile beamed on her face at his words. "So… You do want to marry me?"

Isaiah smiled back at her. "If you will have me."

Happiness overwhelmed Martha. And to think she had been jealous! The Lord was indeed always in control.

"I love you, Martha. Will you marry me?" Isaiah asked.

Her arms flung around his neck in happiness, and she almost fell off the buggy seat. He caught her and held onto her, not letting her slip.

"Yes, yes, I will," she answered, earning a laugh of joy from Isaiah. "And I love you too." She had asked the Lord to create a way, and he had done so by sending a man who cared for and respected her, a man who she knew she would spend her life with doing his works. "Come on, let's go tell my father."

They rode to Martha's house and walked inside to see Barbara and Martha's father reading in their living room. They looked up when Isaiah and Martha came inside.

"We have some wonderful news," Martha said, beaming. "Isaiah asked me to marry him, and I said yes!"

Daed sprang up from his chair, dropping his book and practically knocking over his battery-operated light. "This is indeed wonderful news! I am so happy for you. I pray the Lord blesses you both with a happy, long life together."

"So do I," Barbara said, rising from her seat. "I am happy for you both."

Martha looked at Barbara in surprise as her father hugged her.

"So, Isaiah, what are your plans for building a house?" *Daed* asked.

"Well, there's some land right down the road I've been wanting to buy," Isiah began, and he and *Daed* started talking about building plans for their future home and barn.

As the two men talked, Barbara approached Martha and patted her arm. "May I talk to you for a minute?"

"Of course."

Barbara pulled her aside. "It was me, Martha. I'm the one who spread the rumors about you."

"What?" Martha asked, stunned. "Why?"

"I'm sorry, Martha. That was so wrong of me. And I'm sorry I've been so cruel to you," Barbara said, eyes brimming with tears. "Tomorrow I will go to the elders, confess, and repent so everyone knows the rumors were false. You didn't deserve that."

"I forgive you." Martha reached out and patted her stepmother's arm. "Why did you do it?"

"As I told you before, you remind me of someone. Well, you remind me of myself at your age, but you also remind me of my daughter." Barbara wiped away a tear.

"You have a daughter?"

"No. Not anymore." Barbara paused, looking at the floor. "Not many people know this, but I was in love with a man when I was your age during my *rumspringa*, an outsider. We had a child together although we were unmarried, but he left me when he found out I was pregnant. I stayed away and kept the pregnancy secret, and no one ever knew. She was a perfect little girl. In fact, I named her Martha."

"Her name was Martha?" Martha asked in shock. What were the odds?

"Yes. She died before she was only a few months old in her crib, and I don't know why. No one knew why. After she died, I came back to the community, but no one knew what had happened on my *rumspringa*. The strange thing is she would be your age now. You remind me of her. Every day, every time I see you, I remember the daughter I once had and that I'll never have another daughter again. I'm too old to have any more children now. No one knows about this except your father. I told him about my past, and he still wanted to marry me, so I'm blessed. I'm so sorry for how I've treated you. You've done nothing wrong and didn't deserve it. You just remind me of what I've lost. And I'm ashamed for how I've acted toward you."

"*Maam*," Martha said softly. "I'm so sorry you lost your baby daughter. And I do forgive you. But remember, even though you lost your daughter, you have also gained one. I'm your daughter now."

"Yes," Barbara said, her voice cracking. "I was so angry and sad that I've been blind to that. From now on I will treat you with love, as a mother should treat a daughter. I love you, Martha." Barbara flung her arms around Martha's neck.

Now Martha's own eyes stung with tears, and she hugged her stepmother tightly. "I love you too, *Maam*."

EPILOGUE

That following November, Martha and Isaiah were married. They had a typical simple Amish wedding with no cake, flowers, band or decorations, but it was beautiful to Martha—the wedding she'd always dreamed of. The service was about three hours long with German hymns and a sermon, and at the end, they recited their vows but did not share a kiss, as was normal during Amish weddings.

Every benched was filled with loved ones. Her entire community attending along with relatives who lived out of state, and it was a blissful day indeed.

***

Five years later, a baby's cry was quickly quieted in their new home as Martha cradled him and patted him gently. Martha sang a lullaby as she rocked her second son to sleep.

Their first five years of marriage had flown by, and so far, it had been the happiest time of Martha's life. She knew there were many more good years to come with her husband and growing family.

She smiled as Isaiah walked into the room. He looked tired. It was a wonder they had been able to get any sleep since the birth of their second child, Israel.

"Are you ready?" Isaiah asked.

Martha nodded, and she placed her hand in his as he led her out. "Johnny!" she called out.

"I'm outside!" their three-year-old called from outside.

She laughed. The young couple got into the buggy and headed toward the church.

Martha had been married to Isaiah for five years, and she had never been happier. She was grateful to the Lord for all He had done to bring Isaiah into her life.

Their courtship had led to their wedding, and she would never forget that day. It still seemed as though it had happened yesterday. She'd worn a navy blue dress, white apron, and prayer *kapp* as Amish brides always did in Unity. She had finished making the dress with only a few days left until their wedding, which took place after the publication of their engagement in the church. She had also made dresses for Catherine and Antonia, who had helped her with the wedding.

Isaiah had looked dashing. The wedding had taken place on a lovely morning in November, during the wedding season. Isaiah's father had officiated the ceremony, after which dinner had been served on the first floor of the church. Everyone had brought food to share.

They had lived with her parents for a few months before their home had been completed, as was tradition before moving into their own house. Their life together—it was indeed a blessing from the Lord.

It felt so good to live among the brethren. With her husband by her side, who would hopefully be a minister or elder when the time was right, she felt more of being part of the congregation.

"Have you heard anything more about Jake and Olivia?" Catherine asked, sliding up next to Martha, bringing Martha back to the present with a jolt.

"Yes, I have," Martha said with a sigh. It had taken years for his evil deeds to catch up with Jake. She had long ago forgiven him and had prayed for him to be redeemed and returned to the right path, but Jake had still continued in his bad ways.

Shortly after she got married to Isaiah, he had started dating a sweet Amish girl, Olivia Mast.

Truth be told, Martha had feared for Olivia, and had even offered her friendship. Martha had told Olivia all about what Jake had done to her and had warned her.

But Olivia had refused to listen because Jake had convinced her it was all lies and that he was innocent. She'd been brainwashed. Soon after, Olivia married Jake.

Jake had shut her out from the rest of the community by alienating her. She was ashamed to say it, but Martha had seen how withdrawn Olivia had been. She had seen the marks on the young woman's face and the sadness in her eyes. Several times Martha had pulled Olivia aside and asked her if Jake was hurting her or if Martha could do anything for her, but Olivia had only defended her husband, become more distant, and refused her help.

All Martha could do was get on her knees and pray, hoping the Lord would intervene for her.

Finally, Olivia had stood up to Jake.

Martha had heard that one day Jake attacked and choked Olivia after a trip to the grocery store. Afraid for her life, she'd stabbed him with a kitchen knife.

Jake had not survived the attack. He would never hit another woman again.

Martha still couldn't believe that Jake was dead. Yes, she'd asked God to give him the punishment he deserved, but she never wished death upon him.

The news had spread, and now the truth had fully come to light. Many people in the community rallied around Olivia to support her and understood that she had no choice but to defend her life, but not everyone accepted what Olivia had done in self-defence, and many looked down on her. But Martha understood Olivia and the wrong done to her.

Martha knew Olivia had done no wrong in defending her own life. Last Martha had heard, Olivia had decided to leave the Amish community to become a police officer.

Martha kept Olivia in her prayers.

Isaiah looked at Martha and must have known exactly what she needed because he hugged her.

"I know you worry about Olivia," he said.

"It's terrible," Martha said. "I should have tried harder to convince her not to marry him."

"You did everything you could. Don't blame yourself. God gave Jake a second chance, and he failed to make use of it. We must continue to pray for Olivia," Isaiah said. "The Lord has plans for her future. And now that she is becoming a police officer, maybe she can help other women in similar situations. Maybe she'll make a difference."

"Amen," Martha said, slipping her hand into her husband's. As they rode home in the buggy, the sun beamed down on them, ushering in a new day.

***

Turn the pages for a sneak peek at *Undercover Amish*, the next book in the series, which is about Olivia Mast, the woman who married Jake.

Thanks for reading!

About the Author

Ashley Emma knew she wanted to be a novelist for as long as she can remember. She was home schooled and was blessed with the opportunity to spend her time focusing on reading and writing. She began writing books for fun at a young age, completing her first novella at age 12 and writing her first novel at age 14, then publishing it at age 16.

She went on to write eight more manuscripts before age 25 when she also became a multi-bestselling author.

She owns Fearless Publishing House where she helps other aspiring authors achieve their dreams of publishing their own books.

Ashley lives in Maine with her husband and children, and

plans on releasing several more books in the near future.

Visit her at ashleyemmaauthor.com or email her at ashley@ashleyemmaauthor.com. She loves to hear from her readers!

Looking for something new to read? Check out my other books!

Click here to check out other books by Ashley Emma

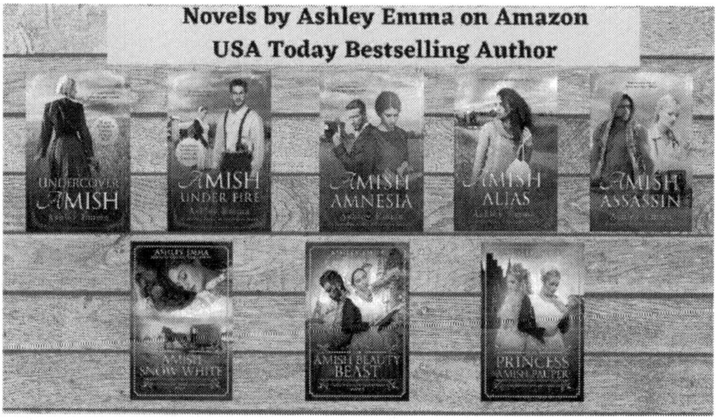

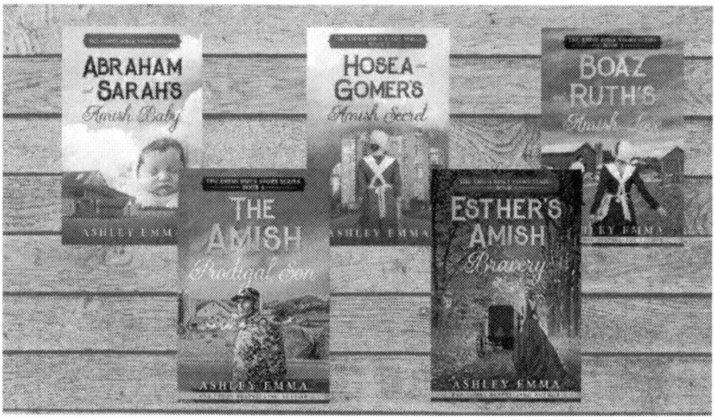

GET 4 OF ASHLEY EMMA'S AMISH EBOOKS FOR FREE

www.AshleyEmmaAuthor.com

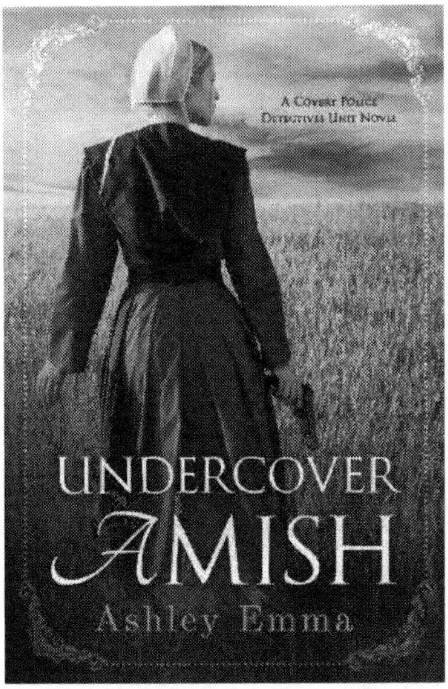

(This series can be read out of order or as standalone novels.)

Detective Olivia Mast would rather run through gunfire than return to her former Amish community in Unity, Maine, where she killed her abusive husband in self-defense.

Olivia covertly investigates a murder there while protecting the man she dated as a teen: Isaac Troyer, a potential target.

When Olivia tells Isaac she is a detective, will he be willing to break Amish rules to help her arrest the killer?

Undercover Amish was a finalist in Maine Romance Writers Strut Your Stuff Competition 2015 where it received 26 out of 27 points and has 455+ Amazon reviews!

Buy here: https://www.amazon.com/Undercover-Amish-Covert-Police-Detectives-ebook/dp/B01L6JE49G

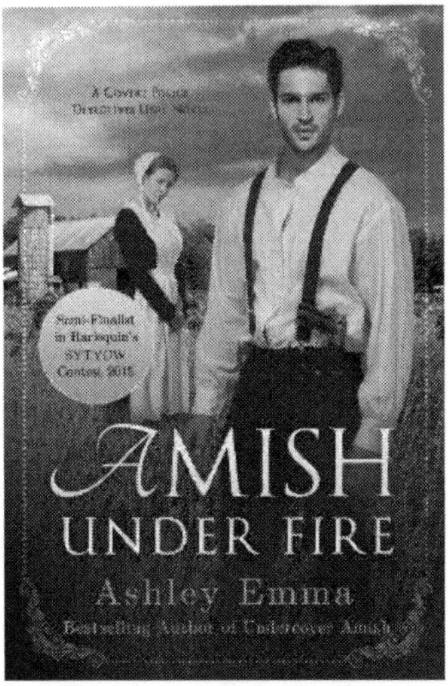

After Maria Mast's abusive ex-boyfriend is arrested for being involved in sex trafficking and modern-day slavery, she thinks that she and her son Carter can safely return to her Amish community.

But the danger has only just begun.

Someone begins stalking her, and they want blood and revenge.

Agent Derek Turner of Covert Police Detectives Unit is assigned as her bodyguard and goes with her to her Amish community in Unity, Maine.

Maria's secretive eyes, painful past, and cautious demeanor intrigue him.

As the human trafficking ring begins to target the Amish community, Derek wonders if the distraction of her will cost him his career…and Maria's life.

Buy on Amazon: http://a.co/fT6D7sM

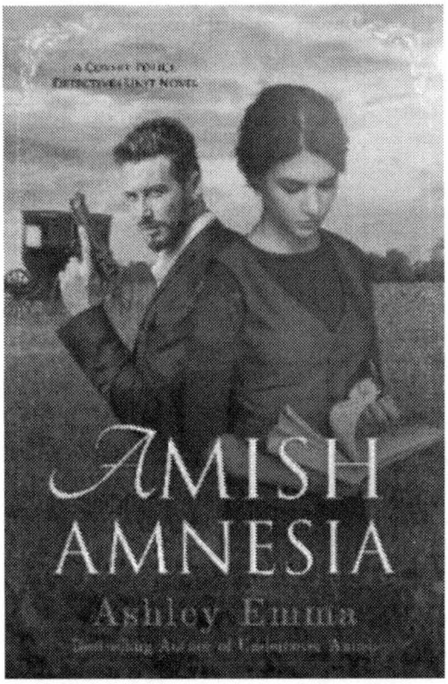

When Officer Jefferson Martin witnesses a young woman being hit by a car near his campsite, all thoughts of vacation vanish as the car speeds off.

When the malnourished, battered woman wakes up, she can't remember anything before the accident. They don't know her name, so they call her Jane.

When someone breaks into her hospital room and tries to kill her before getting away, Jefferson volunteers to protect Jane around the clock. He takes her back to their Kennebunkport beach house along with his upbeat sister Estella and his friend who served with him overseas in the Marine Corps, Ben Banks.

At first, Jane's stalker leaves strange notes, but then his attacks become bolder and more dangerous.

Buy on Amazon:
https://www.amazon.com/gp/product/B07SDSFV3J

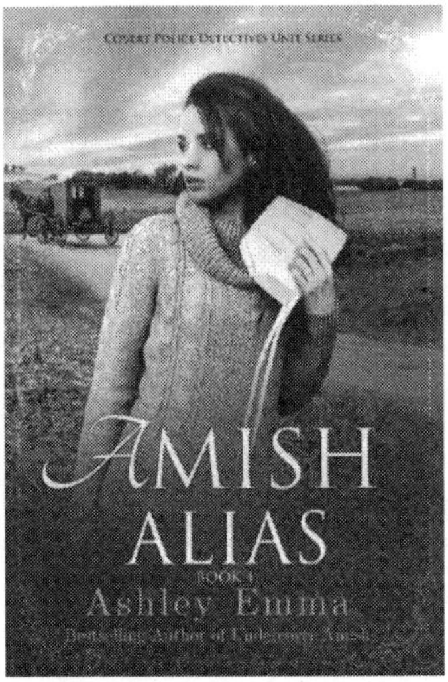

Threatened. Orphaned. On the run.

With no one else to turn to, these two terrified sisters can only hope their Amish aunt will take them in. But the quaint Amish community of Unity, Maine, is not as safe as it seems.

After Charlotte Cooper's parents die and her abusive ex-fiancé threatens her, the only way to protect her younger sister Zoe is by faking their deaths and leaving town.

The sisters' only hope of a safe haven lies with their estranged Amish aunt in Unity, Maine, where their mother grew up before she left the Amish.

Elijah Hochstettler, the family's handsome farmhand, grows closer to Charlotte as she digs up dark family secrets that her mother kept from her.

Buy on Amazon here: https://www.amazon.com/Amish-Alias-Romantic-Suspense-Detectives/dp/1734610808

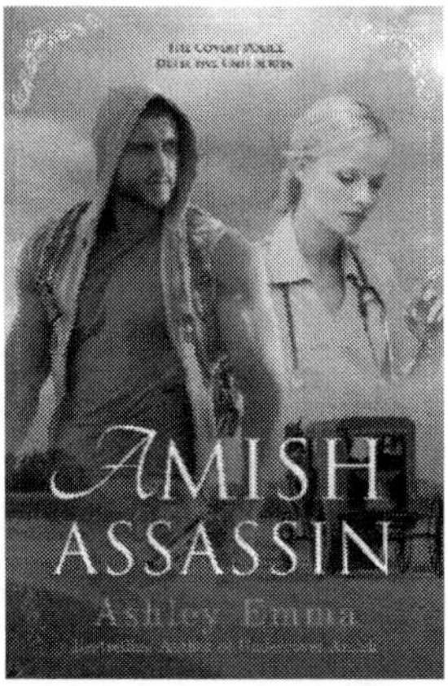

When nurse Anna Hershberger finds a man with a bullet wound who begs her to help him without taking him to the hospital, she has a choice to make.

Going against his wishes, she takes him to the hospital to help him after he passes out. She thinks she made the right decision...until an assassin storms in with a gun. Anna has no choice but to go on the run with her patient.

This handsome stranger, who says his name is Connor, insists that they can't contact the police for help because there are moles leaking information. His mission is to shut down a local sex trafficking ring targeting Anna's former Amish community in Unity, Maine, and he needs her help most of all.

Since Anna was kidnapped by sex traffickers in her Amish community, she would love nothing more than to get justice and help put the criminals behind bars.

But can she trust Connor to not get her killed? And is he really who he says he is?

Buy on Amazon:
https://www.amazon.com/gp/product/B084R9V4CN

Ever wondered what it would be like to live in an Amish community? Now you can find out in this true story with photos.

Buy on Amazon: https://www.amazon.com/Ashleys-Amish-Adventures-Outsider-community-ebook/dp/B01N5714WE

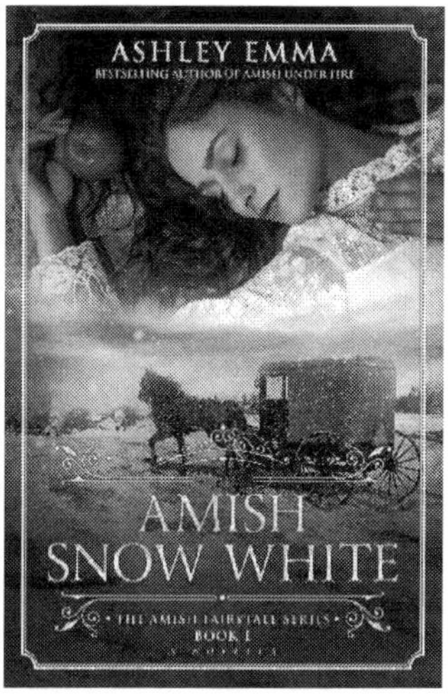

An heiress on the run.

A heartbroken Amish man, sleep-walking through life.

Can true love's kiss break the spell?

After his wife dies and he returns to his Amish community, Dominic feels numb and frozen, like he's under a spell.

When he rescues a woman from a car wreck in a snowstorm, he brings her home to his mother and six younger siblings. They care for her while she sleeps for several days, and when she wakes up in a panic, she pretends to have amnesia.

But waking up is only the beginning of Snow's story.

Buy on Amazon: https://www.amazon.com/Amish-Snow-White-Standalone-Fairytale-ebook/dp/B089NHH7D4

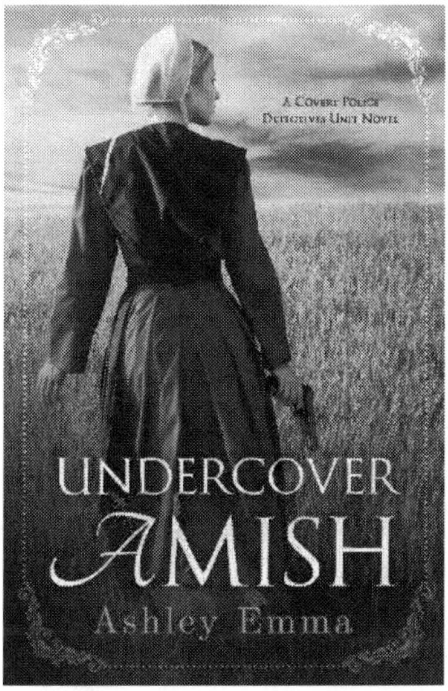

CHAPTER ONE

"Did you find everything you were looking for?" Jake asked.

Olivia Sullivan looked up to see her husband staring at her with furrowed brows and narrowed eyes. The anger flickering in them would soon grow into a hungry flame. He wouldn't yell at her here in the grocery store, but she should hurry to avoid a lecture later at home.

For a moment, she pondered his question. Had she found everything she was looking for?

No.

This was not the life she had signed up for when she had

made her vows to Jake Sullivan.

"Olivia? Did you hear me?" His voice, low and menacing, came through clenched teeth.

"Sorry. I just need to find some toothpaste. I'll be right back."

"Hurry up. I'm hungry and want to go home."

Liv scurried with her basket toward the other end of the store, her long purple dress flapping on her legs. She tugged on the thin ribbons of her white prayer *kapp* to make sure it wasn't crooked and almost ran into her neighbor, Isaac Troyer.

She halted so fast, her basket tipped and her groceries clattered to the floor. "Hi, Isaac. I'm so sorry! I almost ran you over."

"It's all right, Liv. Don't worry about it!" He grinned, green eyes sparkling reassuringly. Then the smile slid from his face and concern shadowed his expression.

Fear swelled within her. Did he know?

She squirmed and avoided his gaze. "I'm so clumsy. I really should watch where I'm going." She shook her head, clearing her thoughts as she dropped to the floor to pick up her groceries. Isaac hurried to help her.

"Really, everyone does these things. So how are you, Liv?" he asked in all seriousness, using the nickname he used to call her when they had dated as teens. They had been so in love back then—until Jake came along and stole her heart with his cheap lies. Isaac was an old friend now and nothing more. The piece of her she had given to him when they had dated died the day she married Jake.

She told herself to act normal, even if he did suspect something. "I'm well. How are you?" She reached for a fallen box of cereal. Her purple sleeve rode up her arm, revealing a dark bruise. She took in a quick, sharp breath and yanked her sleeve down, turning away in shame.

Had he seen it?

Isaac rested his fingers on her arm. "Liv, be honest. Is Jake hurting you? Or did you 'walk into a door' again? You know I don't believe that nonsense. I've known Jake since we were children, and I know how angry he can get. And I know you might be silly sometimes, but you aren't that clumsy."

She sure wasn't silly anymore. Her silliness had also died the day she married Jake.

Olivia stared at Isaac wide-eyed, unable to breathe. He *did* know the truth about Jake. Her pulse quickened as the grocery store seemed to shrink around her, closing her in. Who else knew?

"You don't deserve this, Liv."

What would Jake do to her if he found out Isaac knew?

"Isaac… Promise me you won't say anything. If you do, he

will hurt me terribly. Maybe even—"

"Olivia! Are you okay?" Jake strode over to them. He helped her up in what seemed like a loving way, and no one else noticed his clenching grip on her arm.

Except Isaac. His eyes grew cold as his jaw tightened.

He knew.

Oh, God, please don't let him say anything.

No one would believe him, even if he did. Jake was known for being a polite, helpful person. He was the kind of man who would help anyone at any time, even in the middle of the night or in a storm. No one would ever suspect him of hitting his wife.

He hid that side of himself skillfully, with his mask of deceptive charm that had made her fall in love with him so quickly.

Jake finished piling the groceries into the basket as Isaac stood.

"Good to see you, Isaac." Jake nodded to his former childhood friend.

"Likewise. Take care." Isaac offered a big smile as though nothing had happened.

When Liv glanced over her shoulder at him as she and Jake walked away, Isaac stared back at her, concern lining every feature of his face.

Most of the buggy ride home was nerve-wracking silence. They passed the green fields of summer in Unity, Maine. Horses and cows grazed in the sunlight, and Amish children played in the front yards. Normally she would have enjoyed watching them, but Olivia squeezed her eyes shut. She mentally braced herself for whatever storm raged in Jake's mind that he would soon unleash onto her.

"Want to tell me what happened back there?"

Jake's voice was not loud, but she could tell by his tone that he was infuriated. Who knew what awaited her at home?

"I bumped into Isaac and spilled my groceries. He was just helping me pick them up," she answered in a cool, calm voice. She clasped her hands together in her lap to stop them from shaking, acting as though everything was fine. Their buggy jostled along the side of the road as cars passed.

Did he know what had really happened?

"I was watching from a distance. I saw him touch your arm. I saw the way he smiled at you. And I saw the way you stared at him. You never look at me like that."

Here we go. She sucked in a deep breath, preparing for battle. At least he hadn't heard what Isaac had asked her. Jake was always accusing her of being interested in other men, but it was never true. He was paranoid and insecure.

"You know I love you, Jake."

"I know. But did you ever truly let go of Isaac before you married me? Does part of you still miss him?"

"No, of course not! You have all my love."

"Then why don't you act like it?" His knuckles turned white as he clenched his fists tighter around the reins. "Why don't you ever look at me like that?"

How could he expect her to shower him with love? She tried, but it was so hard to endure his rampages and live up to his impossible standards. Yes, she had married him and would stay true to her vows. She would remain by his side as his wife until death.

However soon that may be. Every time he had one of his rampages, she feared for her life more and more.

She had given up on romance a long time ago. Now she just tried to survive.

If only her parents were still alive… but they had been killed along with the rest of her family in a fire when she had been a teenager. How many times had Liv wished that she could confide in her mother about Jake? She would have known what to do.

"I'm sorry, Jake. I'll try to do better." She told him what he wanted to hear.

"Good." Smugness covered his face as he glanced at her and sat up a bit taller.

When they arrived home, he helped her unload the groceries without saying a word. She knew what was coming. He internalized all his anger, and one small thing would send him over the edge once they were behind closed doors.

When everything was put away, he stalked off to the living room to wait as she prepared dinner. She began chopping vegetables, and not even ten minutes had passed when he stomped into the kitchen. As he startled her, the knife fell on the counter top.

Jake snarled through clenched teeth, crossing the room in three long strides. "You love him, don't you?"

"No, Jake! I told you I don't love him. I love you." She struggled to keep her voice steady. They had had this fight more than once.

"Are you secretly seeing each other?"

She spun around to face him. "No! I would never do that." She might wonder sometimes what her life would have been like if she had married Isaac, but that didn't mean she loved him or had feelings for him, and it certainly didn't mean she would have an affair with him. Happy or not, she was a married Amish woman and would never be unfaithful to her husband.

"I can see it all over your face. It's true. You are seeing him." He lunged toward her, pinning her against the counter top.

She tried to shield her face with her hands. The familiar feeling of overwhelming panic filled her. Her heart pounded as she anticipated what was coming. "No, that's not true!"

"After everything I've given you!" His eyes burned with an angry fire stronger than she had ever seen before. He raised his clenched fist and swung.

Pain exploded in her skull. Her head snapped back from the impact. Before she could recover, he wrapped his hands around her neck, squeezing harder and harder until her feet lifted off the floor.

She clawed at his hands, but he only clenched tighter. Her lungs and throat burned; her body screamed for oxygen.

This was it. She was going to die. She was sure of it.

A strange calm settled over her, and her eyes fluttered shut. It was better this way.

Her eyes snapped open.

No. Not today. For the first time in her life, she had to fight back.

She tried to punch him, but it was as if he didn't feel a thing. She tried to scream for help, but her vocal chords were being crushed. She reached behind her for anything to use to hit him in the head. Her fingers fumbled with something sharp, and it cut her hand. But she ignored the pain.

The knife.

She gripped the handle. Before she could reconsider, she

thrust the knife as hard as she could into the side of his neck.

Blood spurted from the wound as his grip loosened. His eyes widened in shock, and his knees gave out as he crumpled to the floor.

"What have I done?" She inhaled shaky breaths, struggling to get air back into her lungs. Tears stung her eyes. Bile crept up her throat, and she clamped a hand over her mouth. Panic and fear washed over her and settled in her gut.

She had stabbed her own husband.

A sob shook her chest. "Oh, dear Lord! Please be with me."

There was so much blood. Her stomach churned, and her ears rang. Her head was weightless, and her vision tunneled into blackness. She slid against the handmade wooden cabinets to sit on the floor.

She should run to the phone shanty and call an ambulance, but she couldn't move. There was no way she could run or even walk all the way to the shanty without passing out. She would have gone next door to her uncle's house, but her relatives were out of town.

As her vision tunneled, she wasn't sure if she was possibly losing consciousness or dying from being choked.

Either way, she was free.

If you enjoyed this sample of *Undercover Amish*, view it here on Amazon:

https://www.amazon.com/Undercover-Amish-Covert-Police- Detectives-ebook/dp/B01L6JE49G

Or get the entire series here: https://www.amazon.com/gp/product/B08RF3PMLP

Praise for Undercover Amish

"*Undercover Amish* is the first Amish novel I've read, and I have to say it was a fascinating and insightful look into a different culture. Ashley Emma clearly did extensive research on the subject and portrayed this group in a compassionate, thoughtful manner. Couple her careful handling of this society with her compelling characters and heart-racing plot, and you've got a real winner!"
-Staci Troilo, author of *Mind Control*, *Bleeding Heart* and many other titles

"What can I say, I LOVE mysteries! I love getting to know the characters, their motivations and then trying to figure out the outcomes. I am therefore delighted to have discovered *Undercover Amish*. Not only does the main character, Olivia, has a unique background of being Amish, but the trajectory of her life from that background to becoming a policewoman is fascinating and totally unexpected. Not only did I find myself engrossed in the unraveling of a crime, but also in the learning about a culture, within my own country, about which I was, admittedly, basically ignorant. Kudos to Ashley Emma for creating this wonderful series. I can't wait to read more of them!"
-Leslie K. Malin, LCSW, psychotherapist, iLife Transition Coach, and author of *Cracked Open: Reflections on the Transformative Power of Failure, Fear, & Doubt*
website/blog: http://www.JustThinkn.com

"*Undercover Amish* is a suspenseful, realistic work of fiction. Ashley weaves two opposite worlds together in a

fast-paced story following Detective Olivia Mast. Olivia's journey forces her to face issues of identity, rise up to work challenges, and eventually she finds love. It's an easy read that will keep you guessing until the end."
-J.P. Sterling, author of ***Ruby in the Water***

"Buy this book! It's a five-star read in my opinion. Whether you have ever read Amish detective stories before or not, I know you'll like this one and be totally engaged from start to finish. The characters are well-developed, unique, quirky, and three-dimensional. I enjoyed the author giving her readers an inside view of the Amish community, especially during dangerous and unpredictable times. I eagerly await the sequel to this novel!"
-Wendy Pearson, moderator of **The Write Practice**

"I love a good mystery and this one has an interesting storyline. A relatively short read and kept me engaged and trying to guess the next twist. This is the kind of book I love to have when traveling or for an afternoon at the beach."
-C.L. Ferrari, bestselling author of *Enriching Your Retirement*

"Ashley Emma has crafted an intriguing crime mystery with a surprising twist. I didn't see that ending coming at all. And I'm a little jealous. Once I got into this book, I couldn't put it down."
-Michael Wilkinson, bestselling author of *A Father's Guide to Raising Daughters*

"I really enjoyed this book, right through the last page!! Undercover Amish is a compelling read that will keep you

going until the very end! The only disappointing thing for me about Undercover Amish was when the story ended—I already miss the main characters!"
-Sue M Wilson, author of ***Home Matters***
www.suemwilson.com

"This book will take no time at all to grab you and take you into a world most of us know nothing about. Because the author spent time with the Amish, Ashley Emma is able to present her story in a truthful manner. After you read this, you will feel as though you know enough to say you understand them. (You may even find yourself wanting to wear more solids.) But murder has crept into their safe haven. Olivia, the main character, who was once Amish comes back and investigates a string of crimes, all while being undercover. I highly recommend this book. Ashley keeps you on the edge of your horse and buggy seat while making you fall in love with her characters. You'll be sorry once it is over. Thankfully there are more of her books to read coming soon!"
-Emily L. Pittsford, author of A Most Incredible Witness

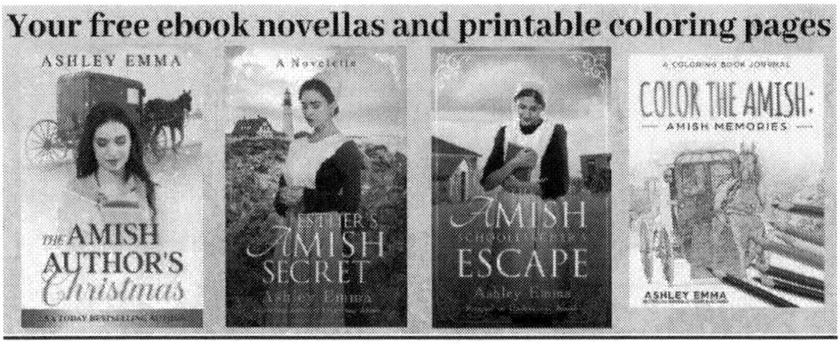
Your free ebook novellas and printable coloring pages
ASHLEY EMMA
THE AMISH AUTHOR'S Christmas
A Novelette
AMISH SECRET
Ashley Emma
AMISH
ESCAPE
Ashley Emma
A COLORING BOOK JOURNAL
COLOR THE AMISH:
AMISH MEMORIES
ASHLEY EMMA

Made in the USA
Middletown, DE
16 April 2024

53075121R10091